The Heiress of Covington Ranch

Samantha Wolf Mysteries
#4

TARA ELLIS

ISBN-13: 978-1522714101
ISBN-10: 1522714103

The Heiress of Covington Ranch

Cover art design Copyright © Melchelle Designs
http://melchelle.designs.com/

Models: Breanna Dahl, Janae Dahl, Chloe Hoyle
Photographer: Tara Ellis Photography

I want to thank my author friends, who have inspired, encouraged, and pushed me to keep growing as a writer. Especially Debbie, who has been my rock .

Samantha Wolf Mysteries

1. The Mystery of Hollow Inn
2. The Secret of Camp Whispering Pines
3. The Beach House Mystery
4. The Heiress of Covington Ranch
5. The Haunting of Eagle Creek Middle School
6. A Mysterious Christmas on Orcas Island

Find these and Tara's other titles on her author page!

http://www.amazon.com/author/taraellis

CONTENTS

1

FIRST DAY BLUES

Sam presses her forehead against the school bus window, looking longingly at the landscape rushing by. Hidden in those trees is a trail that leads to the elementary school, the one she's gone to for practically her whole life. Now, she's forced to ride the bus for the first time and be carted halfway across the county to the central middle school. Not only is it a long ways from home, but it's huge! With over six hundred students, she'll only know a handful of them.

"You sure are quiet."

Sam turns to look at her best friend, Ally, seated beside her. The two of them have grown up together, and become even closer this past summer. They're different in a lot of ways, but their personalities seem to balance each other. At only twelve, they've tackled some pretty exciting mysteries and gotten themselves into some tight spots. Sam knows Ally is anxious about starting seventh grade, too, but she's doing a good job of hiding it.

"Are you wearing mascara?" Sam blurts out suddenly, her thoughts of summer interrupted by the realization that her best friend is wearing make-up. For some reason, this really bothers her.

"Yeah! My mom gave it to me. How does it look?" Patting dramatically at her shoulder-length red hair, Ally bats her lashes and poses for her friend, but her smile wavers when she sees Sam's expression. "What's the matter? You don't like it?"

Sam takes a breath before answering, evaluating her feelings. She notes the stylish outfit Ally is wearing, in comparison to her own plain jeans and faded t-shirt. Not only is Sam's clothes budget a whole lot leaner than Ally's, but she also prefers to be comfortable. Now, looking around at the other girls on the bus, she realizes she might have made a mistake by not taking her friends advice when laying out her outfit last night. Already feeling like she doesn't fit in, her drab clothes and minimal lip gloss are in sharp contrast to even her closest friend. This is going to be harder than she thought.

"No," Sam forces herself to reply, smiling encouragingly at Ally. "You look great!" Tugging at her ponytail, Sam releases her dark hair and runs her fingers through it, smoothing it out. "Maybe you can help me pick out my clothes tomorrow?" she adds, pulling self-consciously at the leather flaking off her tattered sneakers.

"Sam," Ally says softly, realizing now how badly she was misreading her friend. Sam is always the strong, confident one. "You know I'll do whatever you want, but I think you look great the way you are. Not many girls can wear jeans and lip gloss, and still look so pretty."

Although she's never heard anyone describe her as pretty, Sam bites back the first response that comes to mind. Looking up at Ally with her unusual green eyes, Sam knows that her friend is trying to make her feel better, so she just smiles instead of disagreeing. Sitting a little straighter on the uncomfortable bench seat, she focuses on being positive. "Well…maybe I'll make my mom happy and wear the new shirt she bought me. But let's hold off on the mascara. The world might not be ready for that, yet."

Laughing, Ally relaxes, glad to see the old Sam. They're both nervous about starting middle school, and she's counting on her friend to help get them through it.

Turning back to the window, Sam notes that the passing trees are just as desperate as she is to hold onto the summer. Although it's early September, the leaves are still a deep green, without any sign of giving up their perch on the branches.

The foliage abruptly disappears, giving way to manicured fields that surround an impressive, two-story building. Over a dozen school buses are lined up, wrapping around the property, releasing hordes of noisy kids.

Her stomach tightening, Sam takes hold of the hand that Ally offers. Once they come to a stop, they quickly join the milling crowd. Looking around anxiously, Sam tries to remember how to get to her locker. She and Ally had been dismayed at Orientation, the week before, to find out they wouldn't be sharing a locker.

They girls reach the main entrance and hug each other before going their separate ways. Sam feels ridiculous as she fights back tears, reminding herself that she isn't in kindergarten anymore. *I'm sure that I'll make a bunch of new friends,* she tells herself. *I just have to try a little harder, that's all.* But looking up at the passing, unfamiliar faces, they're all just a blur. The hall is so crowded that she has to literally push her way through, becoming desperate to reach her destination.

Rounding a final turn, she sees a strange girl standing in front of her open locker. *It must be the girl that didn't show up last week at orientation,* Sam figures, picking up her pace. Trying to remember her name, so she can call out to her to leave it open, Sam fails to reach her in time. The solemn looking teen glares in Sam's direction before slamming the door and storming off.

Groaning, Sam fumbles with the dial for several minutes before giving up on her memory. Digging into her backpack, she finds the piece of paper with the combination printed out on it. Chewing her lip in concentration, she lines up the numbers in the proper order, and then breathes a sigh of relief when she's rewarded with a loud click.

After stowing her jacket and two large textbooks that she won't need until later, Sam rushes to her first period class, barely making it before the bell sounds. Fortunately, she gets to start her day with what she suspects will be her favorite subject: Art. However, after looking around at what has to be close to thirty other students, she realizes that she doesn't know anyone. Even worse, most of the seats are taken, leaving her with the awkward task of finding a table to join. It reminds her of being alone on a crowded bus full of strangers, with no one offering a seat.

The room is arranged with six oversized workstations, each consisting of a large butcher-block style table and six tall stools. The back tables are full, so she settles on one in the front with only three other kids. They barely acknowledge her as she slips into a seat, the bell ringing at that exact moment. To Sam, it seems

to be a premonition as to how the rest of her day
will go.

2

MISS COVINGTON

The day drags on endlessly, without any sign of improvement. Sam knows two other girls in her second period class, English, but they have assigned seating. Of course, she ends up on the other side of the room from them. Third period, Math, is destined to be, well...*math*.

By the time Sam stumbles into her history class, she's brain-dead and quite literally starving. There are so many students, that they have to break lunch up into two sessions. Much to her stomach's dismay, Sam discovered that she is scheduled for the later lunch, which isn't until after History.

When lunchtime finally rolls around, she's relieved to be waiting in line for food. She holds the typical, hard-plastic lunch tray tightly against her middle, her knuckles white. Standing on her tiptoes, she desperately searches the sea of faces, failing to spot Ally anywhere.

Sam's phone is stowed deep in a side-pocket of her backpack, turned off. Her mother gave her strict instructions to follow the school phone policy and *not* use it until after the final bell rings. If she violates the rules and the phone is taken away, she won't get any sympathy from her parents. Anyway, it's likely that Ally has first lunch, and is now seated in a classroom. If Ally's phone is on, and Sam texts her, it will get them *both* in trouble.

Defeated, Sam sticks the tray out to receive the bland food, and randomly picks a vacant table to sit at. Trying to ignore the fact that her worst school related fear of having to sit alone at lunch is being fulfilled, she daydreams instead of how she plans to spend her free time this afternoon.

The half hour passes blessedly fast, and Sam is relieved when the bell sounds. Her spirits rising, she eagerly makes her way towards the physical education room. It's the only class that she and Ally have together. Different from the PE in elementary school, this one is split between class time and playtime.

In spite of her hustle, Sam still barely makes it there on time, since the cafeteria is on the other side of the campus. Thrilled to see the unmistakable red hair of her best friend seated in the back row, she happily plops down in the vacant seat next to her. They turn to greet each other as the final bell marks the beginning of instruction.

"You have *no* idea how glad I am to see you!" Sam gushes, nearly crying. Her built up anxiety from the day threatens to overwhelm her, but she does her best to hold it back.

"What happened?" Ally asks, concerned. It's obvious that Sam is having a rough time. While Ally was also disappointed not to see her at lunch, it isn't like her friend to make a big deal out of something like that.

"I guess it's just a combination of things," Sam confides. "I hardly know anyone. I'm barely on time to my classes, since they're spread out all over campus, and I sat by myself at lunch."

Taking her hand, Ally gives it a squeeze. "I know you, Sam. I'll bet by the end of the week, you'll be friends with just about everyone. You'll also figure out the quickest routes between classes, and your table will be the loudest one in the whole lunchroom!"

Laughing, Sam's mood improves almost instantly. Ally has a way of saying just what she needs to hear, and she loves her dearly for it.

"Excuse me, girls."

Looking up quickly, a bit shocked by the scorn in the woman's voice, Sam is dismayed to find the teacher glaring at them.

"Please, excuse me for interrupting," the teacher begins, hands on her slim hips. "I'm sure that you're discussing something terribly important, but I find the behavior rude."

There are snickers from around the room, causing Sam and Ally to sink even deeper into their seats.

"Let's see," the teacher continues, looking at a printout of everyone in the class. Sam saw the sheets in the other classrooms. Pictures that were taken at Orientation line up next to student names. "Samantha Wolf, and Allyson Parker?"

"Sam and Ally," Sam says, realizing immediately that correcting the teacher is a mistake. "I'm sorry," she adds quickly. "I was just excited to finally see Ally. We don't have any other classes together. I didn't mean to interrupt."

Tilting her head slightly, the teacher raises an eyebrow at Sam before turning away. Apparently satisfied with the apology, she begins writing out her name on a dry-erase board with a blue marker.

"My name is Miss Covington," she announces, just in case someone failed to read it. Turning back to the class, she crosses her arms over her chest. Although she's barely over five feet tall, she has a presence about her that demands respect. Back straight and shoulders squared, she reminds Sam of a drill sergeant. Her honey-colored hair is meticulously groomed, with a blunt cut at the shoulders, and bangs held back from her face with pins. She's pretty, in spite of her initial, gruff manner, and doesn't look any older than twenty-five or so.

Then she smiles.

The transformation is astounding, and Sam's

first impression is destroyed. Uncrossing her arms, the young woman takes a step towards them, and then leans back against her desk.

"The first day is always hard," she says, looking pointedly at Sam. "But I expect this year will be enjoyable. I have some simple class rules I ask that you follow. I'm going to hand them out, along with a questionnaire so that I can get to know each of you a little bit. These need to be turned back in by tomorrow, and are worth ten points. If you can all handle that homework, then you'll start off with an 'A.'"

Among murmurs of relieved, happy chatter, Miss Covington asks for a volunteer to hand out the papers. Another hand shoots up in the air before Sam can respond. When the girl stands and makes her way to the front, Sam recognizes her as her long-lost locker mate.

As the volunteer walks up and down the rows of desks, Sam struggles to remember her name. She knows they went to the same elementary school for several years, but always had different teachers. The girl was shy and kept to herself on the playground. Sam remembers she was picked on by some of the other kids.

Kelly? No....that's not it, Sam thinks, tapping her pencil. Staring at the girl, trying to jog her memory, she notices how ill-fitting her clothes are. And dirty. Well, maybe not so much dirty, as stained. In fact, it looks like her jeans have been pressed, with a noticeable crease from the iron, but are several inches too short. Her tennis shoes are broken out on the sides, the socks poking through.

"Are you done staring at me? Do I not meet your standards?"

Startled, Sam realizes that the shoes she's gawking at are directly under her nose. Her cheeks flushing, she meets the eyes of her accuser, and the name suddenly pops into her head.

"Cassy Sanchez!" Sam says, unable to think of anything else to say.

Taken slightly aback, Cassy frowns at her. "Yeah? So you know my name. Am I supposed to be impressed?"

Slamming the papers onto Sam's desk, Cassy tugs at a strand of hair that's escaped her ponytail. It's a motion that looks practiced, and Sam suspects it's a nervous habit. While Cassy's clothes are suspect, her long, dark hair is clean and shiny, and compliments her olive complexion.

"I'm sorry," Sam mutters, picking up the handouts. "It's just that we're assigned to the same locker. I was looking at you because I was trying to remember your name. Honest."

Sam glances around, hoping no one else is listening to the exchange. Ally seems to be the only other person interested.

"Well, you sure are apologizing a lot today," Cassy retorts, turning away before Sam can say anything else.

"Don't worry about it," Ally whispers, nudging Sam's side. "She's always been a bit odd. I tried talking to her last year and she totally ignored me."

Still feeling bad, Sam decides that she'll go out of her way to make amends with Cassy. They're going to be sharing the same locker the whole year, so there's bound to be plenty of opportunities.

The rest of the day goes much smoother, and Sam even has a few friends in her last two periods: Science and Social Studies.

Feeling better than she did earlier, Sam waits at her open locker for a full ten minutes, hoping she can gloss things over with Cassy. But as the crowds thin out in the hallway, it becomes clear the other girl is already gone.

Finally giving up, Sam slams the door, spins the dial to lock it, and then heads to the driveway where the bus dropped them off that morning. As she gets closer, it dawns on her how empty the halls are, and she starts to run. Pushing through the outside doors, she sees the final bus pulling around the corner, a small plume of smoke in its wake. The long driveway used for school buses is empty. Only parents in their own cars remain. She missed the bus.

Slapping a hand to her forehead, Sam swings her heavy backpack down onto the ground and finds her phone. As soon as she turns it on, it starts to ring, and she answers Ally's call.

"Where are you?" Ally shouts, her voice barely audible over the noisy kids in the background. "I tried to get the driver to wait, but he wouldn't!"

"I waited to talk to Cassy," Sam explains. "I didn't know that the buses would leave so soon.

How did everyone get on them so fast?"

After promising to text her when she gets home, Sam makes the dreaded call to her mom. She knows what an ordeal it is to get her two-year-old twin sisters into the car. Although not happy about it, Mrs. Wolf promises to be there as soon as possible.

Resigned to waiting, Sam decides to walk around the school until her mom gets there. Kicking at random rocks, Sam doesn't pay attention to where's she going, lost in her thoughts of the wooded trails near her home.

After several minutes, she finds herself in a smaller parking area with a sign that designates it for teachers. Quite a few cars fill the lot, and Sam figures that the owners are still inside working. Her mom was a teacher for several years before leaving her job in order to stay home and raise the twins. While still teaching, she always got home later than Sam, and often continued working at home until late at night, correcting assignments.

Stepping over a curb and onto a strip of grass along the edge of the pavement, movement from a nearby Volkswagen Bug catches Sam's eye. She squints in the late afternoon light, trying to see, then slips into a building's shadow for a better view. Sure enough, there's someone in the driver's seat. The older vehicle is a cute, light blue color and Sam isn't surprised to see that the driver is a woman. What startles her, though, is that the woman is covering her face and her shoulders are heaving. Even with the window up, Sam can hear her sobbing. And what surprises her even more is that it's Miss. Covington.

3

HOME IS WHERE THE HOMEWORK IS

Sam is quiet during the ride home. When she catches her mom looking at her, she rolls her eyes. Her mom always seems to know when something's up.

"I was having a debate with myself over whether I should tell you or not," Sam admits. "I should have known better. You can always tell what I'm thinking."

"Spill it," her mom orders, while checking on the twins in the rearview mirror. "It'll make you feel better," she adds more gently, turning to Sam after coming to a stop at a red light.

Unsure how to start, Sam decides to let her mom in on the first unfortunate exchange she had earlier in the day with her new teacher. By the time she describes the young woman crying in her car, Kathy's frown is deep.

"I know that you don't like having people cross with you," she tells Sam, pulling through the intersection. "And you hate it even more when others are upset, but I really think you need to leave this one alone, Sam. I imagine Miss Covington just had a long first day at school and was simply letting out some frustration."

"Oh, no" Sam gasps. "Do you think what happened with me might have made it worse?"

Laughing, Kathy reaches over to gently touch Sam's arm. "Sam, when I was a teacher, kids talking out of turn was a given. Your apology is more than most kids offer. I'm sure that had nothing to do with her...breakdown. At least, I certainly hope she isn't that sensitive, or she isn't going to last very long."

"Is Miss Covington a new teacher?" Sam already feels better from her mom's reassurance. Her mother joined the school board after resigning from teaching, so she's up on all the new hires.

"Yes, this is her first year as a teacher. But please don't go around talking about it, especially not about what you saw today."

Disappointed that her mom thinks she would do such a thing, Sam chooses her words carefully. "I know better than to do that, Mom."

"Oh, I know you do, Sam," Kathy answers as they head up the long driveway to their house. After parking the car, she puts out a hand to stop Sam from leaving. "Just remember, while I would never make you promise not to speak to Ally about it, because I know that's a promise you can't keep, widening the circle any further would amount to gossip."

It's not like I have anyone else to talk to, Sam thinks. But she knows that isn't the response her mom is looking for. Sam isn't a gossip. She might be nosey and persistent, and sometimes gets involved in situations that are none of her business, but she doesn't go around talking about it with everyone. In this case, though, she knows why her mom is concerned. It would be easy to mention it without really meaning to, while sitting on the bus or at lunch. It wouldn't take much to start rumors, and that could be damaging to a new teacher.

Nodding in understanding, Sam smiles at her mom. "I get what you're saying," she reassures her. "I'll be careful not to talk with Ally about it anywhere that someone might overhear, and I won't pester Miss Covington. Even though we got off to a bad start, she seems really nice. I wouldn't want to do anything to make things hard for her."

The twins are screaming by now, upset about being kept in the car for so long after arriving home.

Apparently satisfied that Sam understands, Kathy turns her attention to the two younger ones. "Hold your horses, girls!" she calls to them, making a funny face. They immediately begin to make poor imitations of horses neighing, and then laugh at each other. It's a well-practiced game that started before they could even crawl.

Sam helps get her sisters out, and then retreats to the sanctuary of her room to get homework done. She doesn't have a huge amount to do, but the biggest assignment is reading the first whole chapter in her history book. Sam likes to read, but prefers fiction.

After trudging through ten math equations without too much trouble, she fills out Miss Covington's questionnaire and then pulls the huge history book out of her backpack.

This is when the twins decide it's time to play. Sam hears them pounding down the hall, long before they reach her room. Taking a deep breath, she prepares to break their little hearts. They fling her door open, a trick they discovered a few weeks before.

Sam looks at the twins' cute blonde heads as they poke them inside her room. Both younger girls inherited their mom's bright blue eyes, while Sam has the same brown hair and unusual green eyes of her father. Sam loves her sisters, and they can normally rely on her to entertain them. But she needs to stand firm in order to finish her homework. "Sissy can't play right now," she says.

Ignoring her, the twins toddle into her room and busy themselves trying to climb up onto her bed. In the midst of grabbing at the soft comforter and scrambling onto the top, they manage to crumple about half of the homework still spread across the surface.

Crying out in alarm, Sam lunges for the papers, trying to rescue as much as she can. Alarmed by their older sister's scream, the twins look at her in shock, scrunching up their faces.

"Oh, no," Sam moans, knowing what's coming next. "I didn't mean it, Tabby and Addy. I'm not mad at you. It's okay!"

Unconvinced by their sister's pleas, their mouths finally open and they begin to wail. Shoulders sagging in defeat, Sam steps back from the bed, the crumpled and torn assignments falling to the floor around her.

Kathy appears in the doorway, expecting to find twins with hurt feelings, and an older sister who's unwilling to play. But when she sees Sam kneeling on the floor, trying to press wrinkles out of the papers, she quickly shoos the twins out. "I'm sorry, Sam," she says softly, noticing her daughter's defeated expression. "I turned my back for a second. They're not used to Sissy being unavailable. I'll keep them in the other room until supper."

"Thanks, Mom," Sam answers. "Think Miss Covington will believe that my sisters ate my homework?" she adds, holding up the torn questionnaire.

Chuckling, Kathy takes the paper from Sam. "I'll go put some tape on it, and add a little note, explaining what happened. I'm sure it'll be okay."

Nodding, Sam stuffs the rest of her work into the backpack and goes back to the history book. She closes the door, wishing it had a lock, and settles back against the headboard to read. After only one paragraph, her cell phone starts buzzing. She has incoming texts from Ally set with a distinct signal, so she knows it's from her best friend. She's eager to speak with her about what happened with Miss Covington, but has decided it can wait.

Glancing at the text, Sam sees that Ally is about to *die of boredom* and wants Sam to come over *now*. Shaking her head and smiling at her friend's dramatics, Sam types out a response. *Gotta finish homework. Will come over after dinner. Have to tell you something!* Her smile widens because she knows that last comment will drive Ally crazy.

Sam again tries to concentrate on the story about ancient civilizations. When her phone buzzes a couple more times, she turns it off.

Trying not to get frustrated, she re-reads the first paragraph for the third time.

"I wanna play, *SISSY!*" Abby suddenly wails from down the hallway. Sam knows that it's Abby, because Tabby doesn't say more than one or two word sentences still.

"Abigail, Mommy told you…Samantha is busy right now. You have to be a big girl and wait."

Listening to her mom, Sam flinches at her formal name. Her parents have a thing for using the older forms of their names from previous generations. It drives her mom crazy when Sam does the whole, 'Abby and Tabby' thing, but it's a hard habit to break. Tabitha, for example, is named after their great-grandmother, who took great offense to the 'Tabby' nickname. So it's somehow considered disrespectful for Sam to use it now with her little sister.

Blinking rapidly, Sam shakes her head, realizing that her thoughts have once again drifted. She is *still* on the first paragraph! *This isn't going to work,* she thinks, slamming the book shut. She glances at the late-afternoon sunshine flowing through her window and comes to a decision. Grabbing her history book, she goes to the back door, slipping on her play shoes. While her 'good' shoes are worn, these are literally falling apart. But they're still her favorites and she refuses to throw them away, much to her mom's disdain.

"Where are you going?" Kathy asks from the kitchen, where she's wrestling the little girls into their highchairs for a snack. This reminds Sam that she's hungry, and she backtracks to the fridge.

"I'm going out to the barn to read," she explains, poking her head inside the refrigerator. Backing out with a drink and cheese stick, she waves the history book in the air. "I just have to get this read, but I'll be back in to help with dinner."

It's her older brother's turn to set the table, but he won't be back from football practice in time. It's Hunter's first day at the high school as a freshman, and she hopes he had a better day than she did. Even though he goes out of his way to torture her, they're only two years apart and used to be pretty close. They've been getting along better since their trip to the beach last month, where he and Ally's older brother, John, helped solve a troubling mystery.

Sam's dad would normally pitch in with dinner duties, but he's in Alaska on his annual fishing trip. He's a career fisherman, and it's the only income for their family, now that her mom isn't working as a teacher. Money is often tight, but his job has been growing lately, with his boss handing him more responsibilities. That also means that he might be away longer. Sam tries not to think about that too much.

Fighting back feelings of guilt over leaving her mom alone with the screaming two-year-olds, she heads to her absolutely favorite place in the world, a dilapidated barn in in the far corner of the property.

Her family's modest, older house sits on a three-acre parcel. Most of the land is behind the home, with a large mowed area giving way to the woods that line the edge of the small town they live in. Her parents bought the property a year before she was born, so this is the only home she's known. During this time, the barn has never been used for anything other than storage, and a place to daydream. Once used for horses and other farm animals, it's now taken over by cobwebs and dust.

Pushing the large, rickety double doors of the barn open, Sam steps inside and breathes in the welcoming scents, a combination of old hay and worn cedar boards. Sunlight filters in through missing planks in the walls, and she stops briefly in the warm beams, closing her eyes and tilting her head up to the light.

Ever since she was a little girl, Sam's dreamed of having her own horse, and adding the unique smells of horse, leather, and saddle soap to the current atmosphere. But she's the only family member willing to put the time and effort into taking care of a horse, and she's always been too young. Now that she's old enough, they don't have enough money to afford one, and all of the necessary care that horses require.

Sighing, Sam turns away from the light and climbs up into the loft. Her dad throws a couple of fresh bales of hay up there every year, since he knows that she likes to use the space.

Plopping down in a well-worn section of hay, she kicks her shoes off and reclines back with the book. "Now, I can concentrate!" she says aloud, enjoying the silence.

Unfortunately, she's sound asleep before even turning the first page.

4

CASSY

The second day of school starts out much better than the first, in part because Sam already knows where she's going and isn't as rushed. Having an idea of what to expect always makes things a little less scary, too.

She spent the time during the bus ride explaining to Ally why she didn't show up the night before. By the time Hunter woke her up by throwing hay on her face, she was already late for dinner. After eating and cleaning up, it was time to help bathe the twins and put them to bed. Sam texted Ally, of course, but that wasn't enough to satisfy her friend. She promised to spend time with her after school today.

Both of Ally's parents work, and usually

aren't home until later in the evening. Since her older brother, John, has football practice until nearly six, that means she's at home alone in her huge house for some time. They often hang out there for that reason, and because Ally has a big game room.

Sam has a nice surprise in first period, when a girl she knows from fifth grade walks in late. Sam waves her over to the empty stool next to her, happy to have someone in her art class that she can talk to.

By the time second lunch arrives, and she stands at the entrance to the cafeteria, her positive mood takes a big hit as she looks around timidly. Sam is determined to find some friends to sit with today. But she'll have to keep her head *up* if that's going to happen. *Not* pointed at the ground.

Taking a big breath, she starts to take a step forward, when someone grabs her from behind.

"Sam!" Ally shouts in her ear.

Sam spins around to face her best friend. "Ally! You nearly gave me a heart attack!" she scolds good-naturedly. "What are you doing here?

"I guess they put a bunch of kids in the wrong classes," Ally explains. "There were close to forty of us in my third period cooking class, so they had to move us around. I now have wood shop. I thought I was going to hate it, but it's actually pretty cool. I get to make a jewelry box for my mom, for Christmas! Anyways," she rushes on, before Sam can get a word in, "The move also changed my lunch period, so now I have second lunch with you!"

They've been moving with the tide of students into the lunch line while talking. Sam picks up a tray, then hands another one to Ally. She can't believe her luck! "This is perfect!" she exclaims, selecting a big slice of pizza. "It makes up for not having more than one class together. And, I won't have to be the 'kid who sits by herself at lunch every day!'"

Laughing, they find an empty table and sit down. Sam doesn't even care if no one else joins them. It doesn't matter now that Ally's there. However, as she takes a generous bite of pizza, she notices Cassy walking by. Still determined to make up for the bad impression she made yesterday, Sam drops her food back on the tray and stands up.

"Cassy!" she calls to the surprised girl. "Would you like to eat with us? There's plenty of room."

Looking hesitantly at Sam, Cassy appears to consider her options. Sam senses Cassy's unsure whether she's being teased or not. She doesn't blame her for being on guard. Other kids have made fun of the unusual girl in the past, and she isn't used to genuine kindness.

"Yeah, come sit next to me!" Ally adds, patting an empty seat.

"Um…okay. I mean, I guess so," Cassy finally mumbles. Shuffling over to the offered seat, she doesn't meet either of their gazes.

Ally and Sam exchange a questioning look, and Sam shrugs. She has no idea why Cassy is so hesitant around them. She knows that Cassy is different, and gets picked on because of it, but she hasn't been around her enough to know just how mean some of the other kids have been.

"What do you have for lunch?" Sam asks, trying to strike up a conversation.

Cassy has a crumpled, worn paper sack on the table in front of her. She's rolling and unrolling the top of the bag, and it's obvious by the condition of the paper that it's been used several times. Slowly, she reaches inside without a word and pulls out a small, soft-looking apple. Next, she places a snack pack of cheese crackers beside it. When she begins opening the crackers, it's apparent that this is all she has.

Sam is shocked. A bad feeling starts stirring within her. She risks being accused of acting rudely again, and studies the girl's appearance. She's wearing the same clothes as yesterday. The backpack she set on the floor is falling apart, with duct tape reinforcing the torn edges. But, just like yesterday, she looks freshly showered. And while the clothes are old and stained, they're still clean.

Cassy is tall for her age, like Sam. In fact, she's probably nearly the same height as Sam, but much thinner. Her face is pale in comparison to her dark hair, and a bit gaunt. She has warm, brown eyes that are slightly sunken, with blackish/purple smudges under them. She has a pleasant face when she isn't frowning, but she doesn't look well.

"Cassy," Sam begins cautiously. "Have you ever considered applying for the free lunch program?"

Pausing with the apple halfway to her mouth, Cassy slams it back down on the table, making both Sam and Ally jump. "What makes you think I need a handout?" she says angrily, glaring at Sam.

The mix of personalities confuses Sam. Most of the time, Cassy comes off as shy and withdrawn. But when she feels she's being judged, she lashes out.

I guess this is how she's learned to protect herself, Sam thinks. Realizing that she needs to tread softly, she chooses her words carefully. "It's not a handout," she says gently. "It's a good program, and a lot of kids use it…including me."

Cassy's expression changes immediately and she stares down at the sad apple in her hand. "Oh."

"I've been using it for the past two years, since my mom stopped working," Sam tells her. "It's really helped, too, because the regular lunch program gets to be expensive. Did you know they also have free breakfast in the morning?"

Looking up at Sam now, Cassy seems interested. "Really? I didn't know that. I never filled out the form. I don't like people to think that…well, that I need help." Her voice trails off at the end, so that Sam and Ally can barely hear her.

"It's not about being needy, Cassy," Ally explains. "Probably over half the kids in here right now are getting it. You go through the same line, and when you give them your ID number, it just shows as paid. No one knows. The form was with your orientation packet. Do you still have it?"

Nodding silently, Cassy twists the stem on the apple until it pulls off. "What do I do with it?" she asks, not looking at either girl.

Encouraged, Ally smiles. "You just fill it out and then turn it into the main office. They'll probably have you set up in a day or two. Can your mom or dad help you fill it out?"

After a full minute of silence, Cassy finally puts the apple back down, and her features soften. "I live with my grandma, and she's not very good at that kind of stuff. But-" Twisting around, Cassy digs in her backpack, then pulls out the form and sets it on the table. "Can you guys…maybe help me?" she asks timidly.

"Sure!" Ally says happily. "I bet you can start getting breakfast and lunch before the end of the week!"

When Cassy's face breaks out in a grin, it completely changes her appearance. Sam is so intrigued by her that she's suddenly overcome with a desire to *really* get to know her. She admires her spirit, and can tell that there is a lot more to her than meets the eye.

"Cassy, would you like to come over this Friday after school, and hang out with Ally and me?" she asks compulsively, not expecting her to say yes.

"Do you really mean it?" Cassy asks. She looks at Sam with so much hope that Sam's compelled to expand the invitation.

"Of course I do. Maybe you can stay the night, too. I'm sure my mom would be okay with it. But I have to warn you, I have two-year-old twin sisters, and a fourteen-year-old brother who will drive us crazy!"

"It's still warm enough out, why don't we just pitch a tent in your backyard?" Ally suggests to Sam, obviously happy with the idea of a sleepover.

"Um, I have to ask my grandma and stuff, but I guess I could stay over. I mean, yeah....I think that would be fun!" Cassy appears excited, but overwhelmed.

The bell rings then, signaling the end of lunch, and the three girls hurry to clear the table. They make it to fourth period with a couple of minutes to spare, and Cassy smiles warmly at them as they part to take their seats.

"I actually like her," Ally whispers to Sam as they take out their assignments from the day before.

Sam carefully presses the creases once more on the crumpled, taped questionnaire, and hopes that the note from her mom is enough to keep her out of trouble. "I do, too," she says. "I think Cassy just needs some real friends."

The final bell rings. Sam holds a finger to her lips when Ally tries to keep talking. She feels like she's on a roll today, and doesn't want to mess it up with her teacher.

The class goes by without incident. Encouraged, Sam decides to offer to help Miss Covington. She knows that her mom had student aides in her class, helping with gathering assignments, running messages, making photocopies, and stuff like that.

Just about everyone else in the class is occupied with the latest handout, labeling the parts of the heart, but Sam has already finished hers. Picking it up, she quietly makes her way towards the front, where Miss Covington is staring intently at her computer screen.

Not wanting to interrupt her reading, Sam walks up behind her and waits patiently. The teacher's desk has two sides to it, and is turned at an angle in the front right corner of the classroom. The monitor is on the side that's against the wall, so Miss Covington's back is to Sam.

Unsure whether to wait or not, Sam can't help but glance past the teacher's head and notice a news article on the computer screen: 'The Eye of Orion Heist.' There's a subtitle, but Sam can't see it. Intrigued, she takes another step forward without thinking, curious to read it.

Sensing motion behind her, Miss Covington turns to see Sam reading over her shoulder. "Excuse me? Can I *help* you?" the young woman says evenly, slapping at her mouse and making the page disappear.

Her face burning hot with embarrassment, Sam holds the handout limply in her hand. This isn't going the way she planned. *Why doesn't Miss Covington want me to see the article?* Sam shakes her head at the thought and tries to focus on her task.

"My mom used to be a teacher, and…um, I mean, I just wanted to let you know that if you ever need any help with anything, that…um, that I would like to help. Not I think you *need* help," Sam adds quickly when her teacher's frown deepens. "I just know that my mom had students help her, and….well, that I could do the same. Help you, I mean. If you ever need it."

A moment of awkward silence passes. Sam's taken a couple of steps back while fumbling with her words, and now stands with her hands clasped in front of her, rocking on her heels. A few of the nearest students have paused in their work to watch the exchange.

"Thank you, Sam," Miss Covington finally answers with a forced politeness "I'll keep that in mind. You can return to your seat now."

Thankful to be excused, Sam turns eagerly to

go. But as she does, she notices Miss Covington reach out to an old newspaper on her desk, and discreetly turn it over. Sam failed to notice it before, but she manages to catch a glimpse at a few of the words before they're hidden.

More than just intrigued now, Sam hurries back to her desk. She's already been waiting eagerly to tell Ally about what she witnessed in the parking lot the day before, and now she has more to add to it. The word 'Orion' was on the newspaper, as well as on the teacher's computer screen. But there was also a name, one that Sam is suddenly very interested in: Covington.

5

WHAT'S IN A NAME?

The computer monitor casts a blue-tinged light on the girls' faces as Sam and Ally lean in close to read the search results. They're seated in the ornately decorated den at Ally's house. The walls are lined with bookcases, and the floor is covered with an expensive oriental rug.

"The Eye of Orion is a rare sixty carat Burma star ruby," Sam reads. "It was originally discovered in Burma in the early 1900's and purchased for $25,000 by a Samuel Covington in the 1930's. Today, its estimated value is approximately three million dollars!" Sam whistles, turning to a wide-eyed Ally. "Wow, that's a lot of money."

"Does it say anything about the heist?" Ally asks, scanning through the rest of the article. She was concerned when Sam told her about finding Miss Covington crying in her car the day before. The teacher really does seem like a nice lady, and Ally hopes she's alright. But this odd twist adds a bit of mystery to the new teacher. How is she related to Samuel Covington? Was she crying because the gem was stolen? Ally knows that if anyone can figure out the answers, Sam can.

"I don't see anything about it here, do you?" Sam replies, still scrolling down the screen. When Ally shakes her head, Sam does a new search, using the word 'heist' in it. This pulls up several other results, and the fifth article down looks like a match.

"This is it!" Sam shouts triumphantly when she sees the newspaper site. "I recognize the banner at the top. Let's see…it was stolen three years ago, out of the home of stock mogul, Peter Covington." Pausing in her excitement, Sam looks at Ally with her eyebrows raised. "What in the world is a 'mogul?'"

"I think that means he's like a big tycoon, or

something. So he's good at what he does, and makes a bunch of money."

"Huh." Turning back to the computer, Sam continues reading. "The estate of Peter Covington has been very guarded with the release of information about the burglary. A public records request reveals that Mr. Covington knew the thief as John Brown, and that at least one family member was involved in the incident. In spite of this, no arrests have been made, nor have any warrants been issued. This leads us to conclude that the true identity of the thief is a mystery, and since the insurance company paid out a handsome sum after a six-month investigation, it's considered a cold case, and may never be solved."

Sitting in stunned silence, Sam feels the hairs rise on the back of her neck…a sensation she often experiences when on the verge of making a revelation. *I'm missing something,* she thinks. Tapping her finger on the edge of the large, wooden desk, she continues to stare at the name: Covington. "Covington," she says aloud, knowing there's a reason her subconscious is fixated on it. "Covington!" she says again, but with more confidence. She goes back to the original search results, and begins skimming through each of them.

"What are you looking for?" Ally asks, knowing that her friend is onto something.

"This!" Sam exclaims. "Peter Covington lives in a town only a couple of hours from here, still in Washington State. What do you think the odds are?"

"What, that Miss Covington is related? I think the odds are high."

"No! I mean, obviously she's related to him. I'm talking about Covington *Ranch*!" Sam is on the edge of her seat now, and she reaches out to grasp Ally's arms. "You know the old abandoned horse ranch at the top of the hill? There hasn't been anyone living there since before I was born, but I've often thought about what it must have looked like back then."

"Well, of course I know the place. We used to go exploring around there all the time," Ally says. "I guess I never paid any attention to the name hanging over the entrance."

Sam can clearly picture the wrought iron, arched entry. She's always admired the fancy letters, and thought the design was clever. Her father explained once that it was the brand used to mark the ranch's very expensive breeding horses. It was a capital C shaped like a horseshoe, with the capital letter R hanging from it at an angle. Many of Sam's daydreams up in the barn loft involved the abandoned ranch, but while she remembers the brand, the Covington name isn't something she's heard for years.

"Do you really think they're the same family?" Ally asks, not at all convinced. "It's been an awfully long time. Wasn't there some sort of horrible accident or something that led to the ranch being closed down?"

Shrugging, Sam turns back to the computer. "I don't know if my parents ever told me why the place was abandoned," Sam admits.

After several more searches without any additional results, Sam gets frustrated. Throwing her hands up in the air, she stands and stretches her back. "I think it's been too long. If we want to search for local stories, we'll have to go to the library and look at the old microfiche." The only reason Sam even knows about the old filing system is because she used it last year to research a paper she wrote about the origin of their town, Oceanside.

"Why don't you ask your mom?" Ally suggests. "I bet she knows, especially since she helped hire Miss Covington."

"I can't," Sam answers, heading for the front door. "My mom already warned me to stay out of her business. If I start asking questions about her past, and about that old property, she'll probably get mad. If she finds out there's a jewel theft tied up in it all, she'll freak out. I can even see her transferring me out of the class, and then we won't have *any* classes together!"

"You could be right," Ally admits, following Sam outside. "We've gotten into trouble more than a couple of times this past summer for snooping into other people's problems. So what else can we do?"

"Go get your bike, and meet me at the end of my driveway," Sam directs, running towards her house.

Less than five minutes later, the two girls are pedaling towards the hill known to the locals as 'Little Mountain.' It encompasses about fifty acres of woods, but only three houses. One sits at the bottom on each side, with the old horse ranch at the top. Most of the woods belong to the ranch, and the fence marking the property line is littered with 'no trespassing' signs that someone put up a couple of years ago. The girls, like all the other kids, used to ignore them, until their parents found out and put a stop to it.

The road, appropriately called 'Little Mountain Road,' is a favorite for sledding, on the rare occasions that it snows. It's also great for a challenging bike ride.

It's been months since they made the trek, and Sam is huffing and puffing hard by the time they reach the top. "Finally!" she gasps, coming to a stop at the base of the arch. The place looks the same, except that weeds along the edge of the long, paved driveway were recently pulled. It's a promising sign.

Ally hesitates at the entrance. "Are you sure about this?" she asks Sam, looking around at the thick woods to either side. It isn't unusual for them to go on bike rides together. Even though they haven't come this way in forever, they can get away with riding up to the ranch without having to come up with an excuse. However, once they cross onto the property, it's a different story. They're doing something they know they'll be reprimanded for.

Nodding, Sam drops her bike near the road. Walking purposefully up the private driveway until the C/R emblem is dangling over her head, she looks up at it and places her hands on her hips. "We just have to peek and see if Miss Covington's car is here. It's the only way to know for sure, short of asking her ourselves," she replies.

"Ask Miss Covington *what*?" a deep voice suddenly shouts from behind them, causing both girls to freeze in fear.

6

ANSWERS ONLY LEAD TO MORE QUESTIONS

Hunter is literally rolling on the ground, laughing. Sam barely restrains herself from kicking her older brother.

"That wasn't funny!" Ally yells at him, but her initial reaction is already fading, and a smile is tugging at her mouth.

"You ... should see ... your faces!" Hunter gasps. He's managed to get back on his feet, but is bent over at the waist, holding his sides.

Sam rolls her eyes at her brother's shenanigans. She's used to it, but it's still annoying. Now that she knows it's only Hunter, the relief she feels is greater than the irritation. His laughter has always been contagious, and she fights to keep from grinning. The fact that Ally is now chortling, too, isn't helping.

"Why aren't you at football practice?" Sam asks, trying to distract him from his original question. "Get kicked off the team already?"

Straightening, Hunter shifts his hands from his sides to his hips, and settles a steely gaze on his younger sister. While their features are similar, he inherited his mother's short stature. So even though he's two years older than Sam is, she's nearly as tall. Based on his current expression, she may have gone a bit too far with her remark. She almost feels guilty.

"No. I wasn't kicked off the team, Sis. Sorry to disappoint. We, meaning the lowliest players on the JV third-string team, got cut loose early so the coaches could focus on the elite. So, answer my question."

"Don't worry, Hunter." Ally walks over next to Sam, and gives her a 'what do we do?' look, before turning back to her brother's friend. "John didn't play any varsity games until later in the season last year. Your freshman year is destined to be spent on the sidelines on Friday nights."

"Nice try, girls," he says mockingly. "But it isn't going to work. What is it you don't want to ask this Covington gal, and who is she? Oh," he adds, "you need to work on your observation skills. I followed you the whole way here and you didn't have a clue."

Ignoring her brother, Sam turns away and starts walking up the driveway. Ally hesitates briefly, but then hurries to catch up, hooking her arm through Sam's.

"Alright," Hunter calls after them. "I guess I'll just go ask Mom."

Stopping, Sam closes her eyes and huffs loudly. "If you're really so desperate to know," she says evenly, turning back to her brother. "Miss Covington is the new PE teacher at the middle school. I got to thinking about the name, and I'm curious if she's related to the Covingtons that owned this ranch," she continues, pointing back at the emblem over the entrance. "I didn't get off to a great start with her, though, and Mom asked me not to bug her. So…" She pauses a little too long here, and can see the suspicion return to her brother's face. "So, we thought we'd just look and see if her car was here."

The three kids stare at each other for several heartbeats, and then Hunter smiles again, crossing his arms over his chest. "Sure. Whatever. Then you won't care if I go, too."

It wasn't a question, and he's already walking quickly towards them. Sam furrows her brow in frustration, but knows she can't stop him. Resigned to the fact that her brother is now somehow a part of this, she turns on her heel and marches alongside him.

"The whole point of this is that I don't want her to *see* us," Sam explains. "So all we're going to do is walk quietly to the end of this driveway, peek at the house, and go back. Got it?"

"I got it," Hunter answers.

Unconvinced that her brother won't cause trouble, Sam guides Ally to the edge of the pavement and under the overhanging trees. Looking back to make sure Hunter is following, they slow down as the driveway widens into a parking area. Once a nice, blacktop circular drive, it's now cracked by intruding tree roots, and overgrown with weeds. The center 'island' used to be a fancy pond and waterfall created with large river rock. It began crumbling years ago, and several small trees have taken root in its remains.

It's obvious that, in spite of the poor state of things, there's been a lot of work done lately. There's a wheelbarrow nearby full of pulled weeds, an old lawnmower on the freshly mowed front yard, and several other yard tools scattered about.

The house itself doesn't look all that bad. It's a massive, two-story ranch-style home with a huge wrap-around porch and fancy shutters. While the siding could use a fresh coat of paint, everything looks intact, and the roof is fairly new. Someone's been taking care of it over the years.

Sam and Ally have never been this close to the house before. They always stuck to the trails in the woods, and didn't have any interest in the estate.

Parked on the far side of the destroyed pond, in front of the main, double-door entrance is the old VW Bug. The blue paint is faded and it's hard to miss the bright yellow smiley face foam ball that's stuck to the top of the antennae.

"That's her car!" Sam whispers excitedly,

clutching tightly at Ally's arm.

"Well, she must not have much money if she drives a clunker like that," Hunter observes, talking a bit too loud.

Shushing him, Sam waves at Hunter and Ally to go back. But as she turns to leave, a flicker of movement catches her eye. Pausing, she looks up at one of the second-story windows, and her stomach clenches with fear as she sees a shadowy face disappear.

7

COLLABORATION

John hasn't showered yet, and his blond hair is sticking out in every direction. His bright blue eyes are the only feature he and Ally share as siblings, and right now, they're fixed on Sam. "So you think that this new teacher might have something to do with a multi-million dollar jewel heist?" he asks, unconvinced.

Sam notices John's left elbow is bleeding, and the knuckles on his right hand are bruised. She didn't realize the football players got beat up so much at practice. Focusing on the question, she tries to decide how to answer it. She really doesn't want to be having this conversation, but she and Ally can't keep everything to themselves anymore, not after Hunter followed them.

"I didn't say that," she replies. "All we know is that she was reading about it and has the same name. I believe there's a good chance that she's related to the stock tycoon who had the gem stolen from him. We need to find out the history of Covington Ranch, and if they're all part of the same family."

"Why?" Hunter asks. He's sprawled out on a large leather sectional couch, with a bag of chips in his lap. This is the only room aside from the kitchen that the kids are allowed to eat in. He always takes full advantage of it. "Why do we have to find out anything? Who cares if they're related? She's just a boring teacher, it's an abandoned, broken-down farm, and that jewel was stolen years ago."

Glaring at her brother, Sam carefully considers her answer. While she told the boys part of what they know, she hasn't talked about seeing their teacher crying in her car. The lecture from her mom on gossiping makes her hold back. She already feels guilty for spying on Miss Covington's house. It's not likely to make a difference in Hunter's attitude, anyway. He still won't understand why Sam feels compelled to put the pieces together. To be honest, she can't really say why, either. Sometimes, she just has to go with her gut.

"I'm not asking for your help," she tells him bluntly. "I'm just curious, okay? I've admired that place for a long time, and now that someone is back living there...I want to know why."

Hunter just shrugs and shoves more chips in his mouth, but John pushes away from the wall where he was leaning.

"Uh huh," he says slowly. "I have a feeling there's more to it than that, Sam, but I'm too busy to help much. Between football and homework, I'm slammed. If anything comes of this, though," he continues, turning now to his younger sister, "you promise to let us in on it. Deal?"

"I promise," Ally says without hesitation. The boys were a critical part of helping them solve their last escapade. Ally is serious about telling John and Hunter if they find out anything remarkable. She knows that while Sam doesn't always act like it, she appreciates their assistance, too.

Looking at the clock on the wall, Sam groans. "I've got to run home for dinner. I'm already late. I haven't even started my homework yet!"

"When can we go to the city library?" Ally asks, as the two of them walk to the front of the house.

"Tomorrow is Wednesday," Sam thinks out loud. "I'm probably going to have to stay home after school so I can get caught up on my work. Friday is the first football game, plus Cassy will hopefully be spending the night. Why don't we ride our bikes there on Saturday?"

In their small town of Oceanside, nothing is too far away. Although the library is on the far end, it's still less than five miles. It doesn't take long to bike it.

"Okay," Ally agrees. "Sam," she calls, holding one side of the double-door entrance open.

Sam picks her bike up, but doesn't get on yet. "Yeah?" she can tell that Ally is troubled by something.

"*Do* you think that Miss Covington is somehow involved in the theft of the Eye of Orion? Could that be how she suddenly has enough money to get the ranch back?"

Shaking her head, Sam throws a leg over the bike. "It doesn't make sense. If she *was* the family member involved, then it wasn't as a suspect. The article said the police didn't have any, other than the John guy who used a fake name. Plus, the insurance company would never pay out if there was any suspicion like that. No," she adds, looking up at the tall evergreens along the edge of the property, thinking back over everything they know so far. "But things don't add up. I'm afraid that she could be in some sort of trouble, and we need to figure out how to help her."

***

The next day at school, Sam is anxious about fifth period. She suspects that her teacher was the person in the window at the ranch and might have seen them. So when Miss Covington calls Sam up to her desk before the end of class, she isn't surprised.

Lisa Covington watches as the tall pre-teen

approaches, and tries to decide how to handle the situation. Sam seems like a nice enough girl, but there's something about her....something different from the other kids. Perhaps she reminds her of herself.

"Were you and Ally at my house last night?" Lisa asks pointedly, deciding not to mess around with niceties.

Sam's eyes widen, even though she was half expecting the question. Miss Covington doesn't look mad, but curious. Nodding, Sam swallows hard. "Yes. I'm sorry for snooping. I wanted to see if you moved into the ranch. Ally and I used to hike there all the time, and I figured your name had to be more than a coincidence."

Lisa taps a pencil against her chin, and Sam can tell she's trying hard not to smile. "So why didn't you come to the door, rather than hide in the bushes?"

Blushing, Sam picks at some tape stuck to the laminate on the edge of the desk. It's a good question, and not an easy one to answer. "My mom told me not to bug you."

Sam is surprised to hear Miss Covington chuckle. When she looks up from her nervous picking, she sees that her teacher is smiling at her.

"Sam, you're welcome to hike on the property whenever you want. My aunt put those no trespassing signs up when hunters began going after the deer. She was concerned for people's safety. Just be careful, okay?"

"Really?" Sam blurts out. "I mean, yeah. We'll be careful," she adds more quietly. "We know most of those trails really well."

Sam can't believe her good luck. Wait until she tells Ally! She turns to go, but Miss Covington puts a hand out to stop her.

"In fact," the teacher says slowly, "how do you feel about yardwork?"

"Yard work?" Sam repeats.

"Yard work. I've got a bunch of it to do, and not enough time or money to pay professional landscapers. If you and Ally are interested in making a little cash, I could really use a hand."

"Sure!" Sam exclaims. This will provide the perfect opportunity to learn everything she needs to know about the ranch, Miss Covington, and maybe the stolen jewel.

"Great. Here," Lisa says, scribbling on a piece of paper. "This is my number. Have your mom call me so I can speak with her and make sure it's okay. If you're free Saturday morning, we can start work at ten."

Taking the paper, Sam's spirits sink. Her mom is *not* going to be as understanding when she finds out Sam was sneaking around at the ranch!

8

A PAINFUL PAST

"How did it go?" Cassy asks as she joins Sam and Ally at the lunch table.

It's 'Football Friday,' and all three girls are wearing their school colors of red and white. Even though the middle school team doesn't play on Friday nights, the younger students still get in on the district-wide school spirit.

Cassy is referring to the dreaded conversation that Sam was putting off with her mom. But in order for her to be allowed to work on the Covington estate, she had to fess up about going against her mother's orders.

"Not so great," Sam replies, picking up a

French fry. "Mom was mad that I went to the ranch, like I knew she would be. She was going to say no, but I came up with a plan she agreed to."

When Cassy raises her eyebrows questioningly, Sam smiles in return. They've gotten to be surprisingly good friends over the past few days, even though they only spend a half hour or so at lunch with each other, and talk occasionally in PE. They seem to be a lot alike.

Cassy's reduced lunch application was accepted, and she started getting the free meals yesterday. Her mood has already improved, and her eyes are a little brighter.

"I suggested that I do the work for free for Miss Covington, as punishment for going on the property. When I told Mom how badly she needs the help, she finally came around. She was on the phone with her for a long time. I think I've been committed to manual labor for the next few months." Sam's enthusiasm slips a little, and she hopes that it'll be worth the blisters.

"Well, at least you get to go!" Cassy replies. "So," she continues, "do you want to hear the story now, or after school?"

Cassy's talking about the family history of

Covington Ranch. Turns out Cassy happens to know a bunch about it, and is eager to share it with them. Sam didn't tell her anything about Miss Covington until the day before, because she's still concerned about being a gossip. But when Cassy suggested that they all hang out on Saturday, after she spends Friday night, Ally slipped and told her they were supposed to go to the ranch that day. Not having a choice, Sam told Cassy how they went up there to nose around. But she doesn't mention the Eye of Orion, or seeing their teacher crying. Much to Sam's frustration, lunch ended yesterday with her being kept in suspense.

Cassy doesn't have a cell phone, and apparently, her home phone has been shut off. So they have no way to talk to each other, except at school. She had to bring a note from her grandma for Sam's mom, giving permission to ride the bus home with them and stay the night.

Sam has been on pins and needles all day, waiting to hear the details behind the failed horse ranch. Now, she turns to Cassy eagerly. "I don't think I can wait another minute!" she breathes dramatically.

Chuckling, Cassy finishes her corndog, and wipes her hands with a napkin. When she starts smoothing out her t-shirt, and fixing her hair, Sam finally punches her lightly in the arm.

"Okay!" Cassy laughs.

Sam notices how much Cassy has relaxed around them in the past couple of days. She never expected her to have such a sense of humor. It's great to see the transformation, and she's really looking forward to getting to know her better. Cassy is one of those people who have many layers, and the first one is the thickest.

"You guys know that I live with my grandma," Cassy begins. "Well, Grams was always obsessed with Covington Ranch for some reason. She used to tell me the same story over and over again, and I'd have to remind her that I already knew it."

"She doesn't talk about it anymore?" Ally questions.

"Grams doesn't talk about a *lot* of things anymore," Cassy states, her face clouding. "Her memory…isn't that good. Back when Grams could still drive, she would always slow down when we passed the entrance to the ranch. Then the history lesson would start. But that hasn't happened now in a couple of years."

Sam wonders about Cassy's home life, but doesn't want to pry. Hearing now that her grandma's health is bad, and that she can't even drive, causes more concern.

During the first week of school, Cassy has only worn two different shirts, with the same small jeans and worn out shoes. It's obvious she doesn't have enough food for lunch, and her health is suffering because of it. If her grandma is the only adult raising her, and isn't well...that would explain a lot.

"Ally! Sam! We didn't know you have this lunch!"

The loud greeting interrupts Sam's thoughts, and she looks up to see two girls and a boy standing beside them. She recognizes all of them as classmates from the elementary school. Heather, the girl that called out, is now looking at them curiously.

"We would sit with you, but it looks like the table is already...ummm...*taken*?" she sneers, staring pointedly at Cassy, and making a show of looking her over from head to toe.

Cassy blushes furiously, and jumps up from the table, stumbling back a couple of steps. "I can sit somewhere else," she mumbles, reaching down for her backpack. "I'm done eating."

Sam clearly remembers a day back in the third grade, when Heather made fun of her for wearing boy's tennis shoes. She had gone home crying, because they were her favorite sneakers, and the wider sizes fit her feet better. After a good talk with her mom, Sam got some markers and decorated them, to make them more unique. When the other kids at school all commented on the 'cool' shoes, Heather never brought it up again.

Now, Sam can't stand to see the same defeated look on Cassy's face. An uncharacteristic wave of anger washes through her.

"Sit down, Cassy!" Sam shouts, slamming her hands down on the table at the same time. Everyone jumps, and several nearby tables fall silent.

Uh-oh, Ally thinks, staring at Sam with wide eyes. She knows it takes a lot to get her best friend mad, but when she does…it's best to get out of her way. Wringing her hands nervously, she watches as Cassy follows the order and sits down without a word.

"You're right, Heather," Sam states evenly, standing up. She's a good three inches taller and even looks down on the boy, Kevin. "This table *is* full. I guess you'll have to find someplace else to eat."

Heather gapes at Sam in disbelief, her mouth open. When Sam doesn't back down, she finally rolls her eyes and flips her long blonde hair over her shoulder. "Whatever, Sam. Have fun with your new…*friend.*"

As the three of them walk away, Sam turns to Cassy. "Don't worry," she says loud enough for the retreating kids to hear. "They're just bullies."

Sitting back down, Sam realizes she's flushed and suddenly sweating. Wiping at her forehead, she takes a drink of water and tries to calm down. The normal chatter returns to the other tables, but Ally and Cassy remain silent. When Sam looks up, she finds both girls watching her.

The girls sit there for a moment, regarding each other in a way that only close friends do. The experience has changed their relationship, much the way playing a sport on the same team does. They're united now, and Sam just made it clear to the whole school.

"Well, *that* was interesting," Ally finally whispers. It breaks the tension, and the three of them laugh.

"Thank you," Cassy says simply. No one has ever stood up for her before, and she doesn't really know what to think about it.

"There's nothing to thank me for, Cassy," Sam says. "Heather is mean. I don't know why she does it, but she's always picked on other kids, including me."

"Sam is right," Ally adds. "She can be nice when she's by herself, but she's different at school. Don't let it get to you. Let's just forget it happened, okay? We're going to have fun tonight!"

Nodding, Cassy takes a deep breath and sits a little straighter. "Still want to hear the story?" she asks, deciding to take Ally's advice. When both Sam and Ally nod, she cups her chin with one hand, and scrunches up her nose in concentration.

"I guess the best place to start is with the

parents. I think their names were Jack and Melissa Covington. Jack got some sort of big inheritance from his father, and used it to purchase the ranch back in the eighties. My grandma used to live here then, but moved not long after they showed up. The ranch was a big deal to the town. There wasn't anything on the hill until they built the place, and it was a huge attraction.

"So, everything was great and all for a long time. The horses they bred and trained were some of the best in the country. Then, Jack and Melissa were on their way to look at a horse somewhere back east, when the charter plane they were on crashed. There weren't any survivors. Lisa was just sixteen at the time."

"How horrible!" Ally exhales, completely caught up in the story. "Oh my gosh," she gasps, making the connection. "Miss Covington *must* be the daughter!"

"Yeah," Cassy confirms. "Grams still has the newspaper clippings. It happened nine years ago, so that would make Lisa Covington twenty-five now. It must be her. She went to live with her aunt after the accident."

"Why would she wait so long to come back?" Sam questions. She feels horrible for Miss Covington.

"Because the house doesn't belong to her," Cassy replies.

"Why not?" Sam scoots forward in her seat, eager to hear the reason. Those hairs are rising again; she knows another important piece of information is about to be revealed.

"This is the part of the story that Grams used to get all worked up about," Cassy answers, glancing up at the clock. They've only got a few minutes of lunch left.

"There were only two other living relatives, besides the daughter; Jack's brother and Melissa's sister. There was some big falling out between the brothers a long time ago, so he didn't get much of anything. The sister was put in charge of the estate. She was left a modest sum to take care of it and their daughter. The parents both had huge life insurance policies, and it was supposed to be put into a trust fund for Lisa. She would get it when she turned twenty-one, and the estate would then be turned over to her. But...," Cassy looks back and forth between the other two girls, drawing out the suspense.

"When the insurance company did their standard investigation, before handing over the money, they discovered that Lisa didn't have a birth certificate. Her aunt admitted that Lisa was adopted. She swore that it was legal, but it was a closed adoption. People searched for weeks, but no one could locate the paperwork. Since they couldn't prove that she was the legal heir, the insurance company wouldn't pay out. It was a big scandal at the time, and in all the papers. Grams moved back here with me about a year before Jack and Melissa Covington died, when I was two. That's why she has the papers. She...likes to keep things.

"Anyways, no one thought it was fair. Everyone knew that Lisa was their daughter, and the intended heir, whether it could be proven or not. But the money has been sitting in a bank ever since, and the property has been sitting empty. Last time Grams talked about it, she suspected that the money left for the upkeep ran out, and the aunt can't afford it anymore."

A hundred questions explode in Sam's head, but the bell interrupts before she can start asking them. However, one thing is certain. The mystery surrounding Covington Ranch is more involved than she thought, and Sam is determined to get to the bottom of it!

9

FRIDAY NIGHT LIGHTS AND A SLEEPOVER

"How about these?" Ally is standing half in and half out of Sam's closet, holding up a pair of blue jeans.

Sam takes the pants from Ally, and looks at the tag inside the waist. "These are the ones!" she confirms, holding them out to Cassy, who is seated on her bed. They already chased the twins out a couple of times, although half-heartedly. They don't really mind having the younger girls around.

"Are you sure?" Cassy asks, taking the jeans. She holds them somewhat awkwardly, unsure what to do with them.

Sam came up with the idea earlier, knowing she's a little taller and slightly heavier than the other girl. It made sense that her clothes from the year before might be the right size. Hoping she wouldn't offend Cassy, Sam offered to go through the clothes after school. Fortunately, Cassy seemed okay with it.

"Of course, I'm sure!" Sam replies. "I would still be wearing them, except I grew too much. If you don't want them, my mom's just going to give them to the church for their annual yard sale. They're still in good shape. Here," Sam continues, stepping into the closet with Ally. She tosses out a few shirts, and then a pair of shoes. "Those are all the things my mom had me sort through. I would much rather give them to a friend."

Cassy's face brightens at the word 'friend,' and she leans over to gather up the other items.

"Try them on!" Ally prompts. "The bathroom is right across the hall."

When Cassy comes back minutes later, she is beaming with delight. Everything fits perfectly, and she even makes a little turn to show it off.

"Let's go to my house next!" Ally announces. "None of my clothes will fit either one of you," she laughs, "but I told Sam I'd give her a makeover. My mom got me some new make-up. Why don't we all do it?"

The three girls trample down the hallway, but Kathy stops them before they make it outside. "Whoa!" she hollers, appearing in front of the door, blocking their way. "Where are you all off to?"

"We're going to Ally's house for a little bit, Mom," Sam says happily. "Do you need us to do anything before we go?"

"I think it'd be a good idea to set up the tent now, before it starts getting dark. And we have to leave right after dinner, by six, in order to make it to the football game on time. Oh," Kathy adds, turning her attention to Cassy. "The clothes look good on you!"

"Thank you, Mrs. Wolf," Cassy replies politely.

Kathy nods in approval at Sam's respectful new friend before refocusing on her daughter. "I'm going to need help with dinner, too, so you need to be back here by five."

"Okay, Mom." Sam steps around her and opens the door. "We'll get everything set up first. Where's the tent?"

"It should be in the garage, with all of the other camping gear," Kathy calls over her shoulder, on her way back to the kitchen where the twins are having another snack.

Sam could swear her sisters have about ten snacks a day. Life must be tough being a two-year-old. Her stomach grumbles at the thought and she hesitates in the doorway. But before she can ask her friends if they're hungry, her mom reappears and throws a bag of cookies at her. Sam catches it mid-air and smiles appreciatively before stepping outside.

Three hours later, they're all piled into the Wolfs' van, on their way to the football field. The twins were dropped off at a sitter, since Kathy wants to actually watch the game, rather than chase the little girls around the whole time.

Sam got the coveted shotgun seat, due to winning a game of rock-paper-scissors. Now she glances at herself in the small mirror on the visor. She didn't get her makeover. Looking towards the driver's side, she grins. Her mom knew all along that it was going to take them forever to get that tent put up. *She's a smart lady,* Sam thinks, turning back to the mirror. *And always one step ahead of me.*

It's questionable whether the tent will still be up by morning, but it's not supposed to rain, so Sam isn't concerned. They're sure to have fun no matter what.

Pulling into the parking lot, Sam spots Lisa Covington's blue VW Bug. "Hey! Miss Covington is here," she calls to her friends in the back seat. "If we find her, we can ask about Cassy coming to the ranch tomorrow. I'm sure she'll be fine with it."

They spent some time discussing the ranch earlier, while struggling to put the tent together. Since Cassy was turning out to be a vital source of information regarding the Covington family, Sam figured it would be smart to let her in on everything. Cassy listened to Sam and Ally's speculation about the Eye of Orion, and then the discovery of Miss Covington crying in her car. After several long minutes of quiet speculation, she simply nodded her head.

"You're right, Sam," Cassy agreed.

"Something weird is going on. I'd love to help you figure it out."

It was that easy. Now, the three of them are committed to helping Lisa Covington fix up the ranch, *and* hopefully get to the bottom of whatever else she's mixed up in.

This isn't the first high school football game Sam has been to, but she's never seen her brother play. She probably won't tonight, either, since he's on junior varsity, but John will be playing a lot.

Ally sits on the edge of the wooden bleachers, wringing her hands nervously. It always worries her when John steps out on the field. Unlike Sam and Hunter, she and John have always gotten along. Maybe it's because there's a bigger gap in their age, with him being sixteen and her twelve, but she's always looked up to him. Craning her neck to see him in the line-up, she finally spots him.

"There's John!" she shouts, pointing. "He's the first one on the far side. I think that spot is called the tight end."

"Are your parents able to make it?" Sam's mom asks, frowning slightly. She's never quite understood how Ally's parents can miss nearly all of the school activities.

"Dad might get here later," Ally replies, not taking any offence to the question. "He usually gets stuck in the Friday night rush hour traffic. Mom's working a swing shift at the hospital right now. She probably won't get home until midnight."

Cassy glances back and forth between them all as they talk, unsure of the family dynamics. She isn't used to having a mother figure around. She can tell that Mrs. Wolf doesn't approve of Ally's parents' absence, but it appears to be an expected occurrence. Cassy would give anything just to *have* parents.

The first half of the game flies by, and they all get caught up in the cheering and excitement. Sam is hoarse by halftime, so the girls go in search of something to drink. Her mom gives them money to bring her back a coffee from the concession stand.

"Do you think John will be okay?" Cassy asks as they make their way back towards the stands. He took a hard hit on the last play and was slow to get up.

"He's always getting beat up, but he'll be fine," Ally reassures her. "Hey!" she suddenly shouts, pointing into the nearby parking lot. "Isn't that Miss Covington? I think she's leaving!"

They've gotten halfway up the bleachers, so Sam has a clear view of the parking lot spread out below them. Sure enough, Lisa is standing next to the blue car, visible under the bright, fluorescent lights. She looks to be holding the door open, while turning away from it and towards a man standing a short distance away.

Sam leads the way as they rush back down the steep steps and towards the parking lot, hoping they can catch her. Sam doesn't want to be rude and show up with someone extra the next day without her teacher's approval. It would be easy enough for Cassy to go home after the sleepover, but it would be awkward to not invite her along.

As they run single-file through the exit in the chain-link fence, the lights pop on in Miss Covington's car and it roars to life. They aren't going to make it. Sam considers throwing her arms up in the air to try to catch her attention, but then she notices that the man she saw earlier is stepping out in front of the car!

Skidding to a stop, both Ally and Cassy crash into Sam and all three of them nearly topple to the ground.

"Why did you stop?" Ally demands, catching Sam by the arms to steady herself.

"Look!" Sam directs, whispering now. "Who do you think that could be?"

The tall man in question is standing squarely in Miss Covington's headlights with his hands on his hips. He has very broad shoulders and an imposing figure.

"You can't keep avoiding me, Lisa!" the man shouts, loud enough so that the girls can just make out what he's saying. It's hard to tell how old he is.

Sam is debating whether to step out of the shadows of the bleachers, when Lisa puts the car in gear and speeds forward! The man jumps out of the way as she swerves around him, her tires squealing on the way out of the parking lot.

Ally and Cassy look at Sam in astonishment, but she is already in motion. Putting an arm around each of them, she quickly leads them back towards the game. Something tells her they don't want to meet this mystery man...*yet*.

10

UNCLE PETE

The road to the ranch seems much steeper on Saturday morning, probably because none of the girls got a whole lot of sleep the night before.

"Slow down, Sam!" Ally gasps, peddling as hard as she can. She and Cassy are a good fifty feet behind Sam now. While Ally is on a nice ten-speed, Cassy is on John's old mountain bike, which only has three gears. Ally has no idea how she's even still moving.

It was decided that Cassy should just go with them, and risk having Miss Covington say no. It's unlikely that she'll even care.

"If...I...slow down," Sam calls back over her

shoulder, 'I'll never make it!'"

Finally, they reach the crest of the hill and it flattens out, and Sam coasts until the other two girls catch up to her. They're all out of breath and a bit flushed, but still in good spirits.

Last night was a lot of fun. They stopped at Ally's on their way back from the game so she could get her make-up, and they did their makeovers by flashlight. Needless to say, the results were less than stellar, but none of them cared. They were laughing until well past midnight, when Hunter and John sprayed the tent with a hose. This led to a water-fight that Sam's mom was *not* happy about.

The combination of thick, poorly applied eyeliner and mascara wasn't a good mix with the water. Sam spent ten minutes this morning trying to wipe the streaks off her cheeks, which she only discovered after going inside. Now, looking at Ally and Cassy, she muffles a giggle. They both look like they've been in a boxing match.

They come to a stop at the entrance to the private drive, and form a line across the road. Ally takes a long gulp from her water bottle, and then offers it to Cassy, who takes it thankfully.

"I'm already beat," Ally states. "We should have gone to bed earlier so we'd be able to get more work done."

"I doubt she'll have us doing anything too horrible," Sam counters. Checking her watch, she sees that they're a little early. Leaning back on her seat, she studies the archway. "So you still think that guy last night is some long-lost love?" She's directing her question to Cassy. They had debated the topic for some time while huddled in their sleeping bags.

"Why else would she be avoiding him?" Cassy replies. "Maybe it's even why she moved back here."

"I still say he sounded too old," Ally adds.

"I guess we could just ask her," Sam decides, pedaling again.

Before they reach the point where the road broadens and then wraps around the broken waterfall, they begin to hear voices. One is clearly Miss Covington's and the other belongs to the same man from the parking lot! It sounds like a heated discussion, and as they continue to get closer, the words become distinguishable.

"I told you before that you can't *come* here!"

Lisa says, obviously upset. "I don't know why you insist on following me around. Just leave me alone!"

"My dear, I simply want to go through some of my brother's things. If you insist on being…difficult, then we can do things the *hard* way." His voice drops a little lower, so that the menacing tone can't be missed.

While Ally and Cassy hesitate, Sam suddenly pedals harder and boldly rides around the expensive sedan sitting in front of the house. Loose dirt sprays out from under her back tire as she brakes hard, coming to a stop in between Miss Covington and the mystery man. Only, it isn't a mystery anymore to her.

"Peter Covington!" Sam shouts, surprising even herself with the strength in her voice.

The older man takes a hesitant step back, confused by the sudden appearance of the girl. He quickly regains his composure, however, and turns his grey, steely eyes on Sam.

"And who might *you* be?" he asks, looking at her with disdain.

"*We* are friends of Miss Covington's," Sam answers, nodding at Ally and Cassy as they make their way to her side. Twisting on her seat, she looks at the startled woman behind them. "Are you okay?" she asks. "Do you need us to call someone?"

"There's no point in involving anyone else," Peter Covington spits out, opening his car door. "This is a private family matter, and no one else's business. Remember that," he says coolly, glaring at his niece and pointing a long finger in her direction. "I can make things very difficult for you." With that, he gets into his car with a flourish and speeds up the driveway, leaving them all staring after him in shocked silence.

"I'm sorry you had to be a part of that," Miss Covington moans after he's gone, sitting down hard on the porch steps behind her. Placing her face in her hands, she takes several deep breaths, trying to steady herself.

"It's okay, Miss Covington." Sam gets off her bike and goes to sit next to the young woman. "It isn't your fault."

"Oh…but it *is*," she says with a humorless laugh, dropping her hands away. She stares at the three girls and seems to come to a decision. "You may as well call me Lisa while you're here.

Otherwise, I'm going to feel like an old maid."

"Miss—I mean, Lisa," Ally says softly. "Are you really living here all by yourself?"

Lisa opens her mouth to answer, but then she pauses, her eyes widening, and turns instead to Sam. "How in the world did you know that he was my uncle?" she demands, sounding a bit suspicious.

"Umm…" Sam drawls, thinking hard to come up with an honest answer. When she can see no other way but to confess, her shoulders drop and she stares down at the ground. "I saw what you were reading on the computer the other day, and then the newspaper article on your desk. I was curious, so I looked up the Eye of Orion and figured that Peter Covington must be a relative of yours, and I saw a picture of him."

"So *that's* why you came poking around out here," Lisa surmises, sounding impressed, rather than angry.

Sam peers up at her cautiously, and is encouraged by the pleasant expression she sees on Lisa's face. Nodding once in confirmation, she glances over at Cassy and Ally, who both appear relieved by their teacher's reaction.

"Why is your own uncle being so mean?" Cassy asks, sitting down next to Sam.

"Cassy, right?" Lisa asks while standing and brushing her hands on her jeans.

"Cassy stayed over last night, and wanted to help you, too," Sam explains. "I hope you don't mind her coming with us."

Shaking her head no, Lisa puts her hands on her hips and regards her three students. "It's fine if you all want to stay. And yes, Ally, I'm all alone here, so I appreciate the assistance as long as your parents are all on board with it. As for my uncle…it's complicated. But…" Rubbing her hands over her eyes, she takes yet another deep breath. "I think you deserve an answer."

Picking up a nearby shovel, Lisa slams the point into the ground and then leans on the handle. "I suppose we're already past the point of having what I would consider an ill-advised personal relationship between a teacher and students. I would never ask you to keep anything from your parents, but I *am* going to request that you not speak about any of this with other students at the school. Okay? It could cause some issues that I'd rather not deal with."

All three girls nod in agreement, and Lisa continues, uninterrupted.

"My father and uncle had a huge falling out when I was a little girl, and I hardly saw my uncle while growing up. After the... umm... accident, he came around a few times, but then disappeared again shortly after they died. I assume you know about my parents?" When no one presses for more information, she understandably jumps ahead in her story.

"My aunt took care of me, and helped me get into a good college. While there, when I was twenty-two, I met a boy. He showered me with attention and took me to a couple of fancy restaurants. On the third or fourth date, he started asking me questions about my uncle, who was in all the papers for his stock market feats. John, the man I was dating, was a business major. Or so he claimed."

Closing her eyes, Lisa rubs at her temples as if a headache is starting. "I was swooning over him, and would have done anything to make him happy. So when he asked me if I could arrange a dinner with my uncle, his idol, I said yes, of course. To my surprise, my uncle agreed to it, and even seemed glad to have reconnected again.

"The first dinner at Uncle Peter's house was magnificent. I'd never been in such a grand house, and it was easy to picture myself in a similar mansion, with John as my husband." Snorting, she stands back from the shovel and then tosses it aside, shaking her head.

"Uncle Peter suggested a second dinner the following weekend, and I was so happy! Everything seemed to be going well. But then…that night, as my uncle and I were speaking in his den after supper, John excused himself to use the bathroom. It was only a few minutes later that an incredibly loud alarm pierced the air. I had *no* idea what was happening, of course, but my uncle ran frantically from the room.

"You see, he kept our prized family heirloom, The Eye of Orion, under a glass case in the library, at the other end of the house. While the estate itself was well protected to keep people out and away from the rare gem, he hadn't planned adequately for an *inside* attack.

"John Brown wasn't the man's real name. The police weren't able to determine who he really was, as he was careful not to leave any prints. He was using me. And I allowed it. I thought my uncle was being gracious at the time, by demanding my name not be included in the official findings of the investigation. But I soon came to realize that it was more about trying to save himself from the embarrassment of having his own family involved in the heist."

"But you didn't know!" Sam points out, feeling horrible for Lisa.

"Of course not, and the police saw that right away, thankfully. But my uncle stopped talking to me again. This past week is the first I've heard or seen of him in nearly three years."

"What brings him back now?" Ally asks, caught up in the story.

"He's demanding to be let onto the property, to go through my father's things. But my aunt, who owns the house, has forbidden him from stepping foot on the estate," Lisa explains. "According to Aunt Clara, who is my mom's sister, he behaved despicably during the week following the reading of my parents' wills. I don't know what happened, but my aunt has been adamant ever since that he have nothing to do with Covington Ranch. I don't know why he's threatening to blame the theft on me now, but he's using it to try and circumvent my aunt's authority and gain access to the house."

"What about getting a restraining order against him?" Sam suggests, even though she has no idea what that would involve.

"Sam, while I know I didn't have anything to do with the Eye of Orion being stolen, if my uncle went to the police suggesting that I *did*...something like that could ruin my career."

"I think," Sam states, as she stands and walks over to Lisa, "That the best thing you could do is figure out what it is he's looking for. And we can help you!"

11

COVINGTON RANCH

Chuckling, Lisa puts a hand on Sam's shoulder. "Sam, I appreciate your enthusiasm, but I don't think there's much of a mystery here. I've heard that you and Ally have a knack for figuring things out, and I can see why! I'm sorry to disappoint you, but my uncle is right. It's just a long-seated family quarrel that's never made sense to me."

Unconvinced, Sam tries again. "He sure seemed eager to get inside, though. What do you…"

Removing her hand, Lisa puts it palm up in front of Sam's face and effectively stops her from speaking. "It's a power struggle between him and my aunt. That's all. For whatever reason, my coming back here to the ranch has gotten him all worked up. If he keeps at it, I'll talk to Aunt Clara, but I'd rather not. She gets very upset over any conversation involving him."

Ally casually glides up next to Sam and throws an arm around her shoulders. It's a perfectly normal embrace they often share, but it's also Ally's way of heading things off. She knows Sam too well, and she subtly takes control of the conversation before Sam pushes too far.

"Don't worry," Ally assures Lisa. "We would never talk about your personal family stuff with other kids. I hope he'll leave you alone. So, what made you come back to the ranch?"

The change in subject has the desired effect, and puts their teacher at ease. Lisa retrieves the shovel with a lighter step. "I wish it were because I was coming home to stay," she answers, sounding nostalgic.

Handing the shovel to Ally, she then directs Sam to get the wheelbarrow, and Cassy a rake laying nearby.

"Unfortunately, it's to fix the place up to sell

it," Lisa says, sighing.

"What?" Cassy grips the rake close to her chest. "Why would you do that?"

"It's not because I want to," Lisa explains. "My parents left the estate and what cash they had in savings to my aunt. There was...an issue with my inheritance, which is how my parents would have expected me to keep Covington Ranch operational. Well, that didn't happen. Instead, I barely had enough to go to college, and still keep the house from falling apart.

"After paying the property taxes for almost ten years, we're simply running out of money. Even though there isn't a mortgage, since it was owned when my aunt inherited it, there are still bills every month. Do you know how much it costs for property insurance on a place like this?"

Of course, none of the girls have a clue how much property tax or insurance is, so they just shrug in response.

"Well, it's a lot," Lisa states, waving a hand to encompass the two-story, custom-built house in front of them. In addition to the wrap-around porch, its cedar siding and dual bay windows to either side of the double door entry give it an expensive, yet cozy appearance.

"Even living here rent-free," Lisa continues, still staring at the house, "I can't afford the upkeep on my teacher's salary. So we have no other choice but to sell it."

"How many acres do you have?" Ally asks. "Could you sub-divide and sell some of it?"

Lisa turns to study Ally for a moment before answering. The small, red-headed girl is smart for her age. "That's a very intelligent suggestion, Ally," she finally says. "Out here in the county, the zoning limits the lots to no less than twenty acres. So you are right that we could break it up into three other lots and try to sell them. However, the process involved in surveying and dividing the land would take the rest of the money, and we have no guarantee if or when the other lots might sell. I'd be left without any way to pay for the taxes or improvements that the place needs. My aunt and I decided it was too great of a risk.

"This is the last connection I have left to my parents. I came by a few times before, when I was on break from school, but it's always been too painful to stay for very long. But now that

I'm faced with losing it forever…well, I guess I just always thought it would be here, and now I wish I had come back sooner."

"I know what it's like to not have your parents," Cassy says, her voice low.

Cassy has said so little about how she came to live with her grandma, that Sam and Ally really don't know anything about her past. Sam's instinct is to go hug her, but she holds back, afraid that it will keep Cassy from saying what she obviously has on her mind.

"I'd give anything to have a home that was filled with their memories," Cassy says. "But I've only got a box with some news clippings and pictures."

Lisa is surprised by the young girl's revelation. Although some might take her statements as looking for sympathy, it's clear from Cassy's expression that she's just being honest.

Lisa notices the new set of clothes she's wearing, her loose hair, and day-old makeup. Cassy is one of those students that she was warned about. The kind that you *know* needs help, but giving it would mean getting too involved. Lisa is relieved and impressed that Sam and Ally have taken her in as a friend.

"Cassy," Lisa replies gently. "Your box of memories is precious, and more than some people have. I think the best we can do is to try to remember our parents, and honor them in how we live our lives."

Nodding silently, Cassy brushes away a tear before lowering her rake. "Where should we start?" she asks, putting a clear end to the conversation.

"I've gotten a good start on pulling weeds and trimming the bushes, but I left the remnants all over the place," Lisa explains, happy to get to work. "So how about you go around and fill the wheelbarrow with it, and then I'll show you where I've been dumping everything?"

As the four of them scatter in search of yard waste, Sam's mind is still turning everything over. *Am I wrong?* Sam asks herself, picking up a branch. *Is there really nothing here to solve?* Straightening, she slowly looks around her at the surrounding woods, and then finally back at the house. She pictures the Eye of Orion, and the angry face of Peter Covington. *Lisa can't lose*

Covington Ranch! Sam decides, throwing the branch into the wheelbarrow. *And I'm going to find a way to save it.*

12

GRAMS

Sam and Ally insist on riding home with Cassy. It's starting to get dark by the time they finish for the day, and they don't want her riding alone. It's easy enough for them to go in a big loop to get back to their neighborhood as it's not much farther. John told Cassy earlier that she could just keep the bike, which is too small for him now, anyway.

Time passes quickly while working around the ranch. The weeds appear to be endless, and most of the grounds are overgrown. The girls promised to help every day after school, so long as they don't have too much homework. Sam is secretly hoping it might help their workload in Miss Covington's class, but she isn't holding her breath.

It takes less than twenty minutes to reach Cassy's road, and she comes to a stop under the street sign. They're in a rural area, so there aren't many houses on the block.

"I'm fine from here," Cassy says nervously, glancing down the street.

It's obvious to Sam that she doesn't want her new friends to see where she lives, and that worries her. "Can we come in for a minute with you, Cassy? I really need to use a bathroom, and I would love to meet your grandma." She knows she's being pushy, but something tells her that she needs to see inside the house.

Shifting uneasily from foot to foot, straddling the high bar on the boy-style bike, Cassy appears almost frightened. "I don't think that's a good idea," she nearly whispers. "Grams doesn't do great with unplanned company."

"Cassy," Ally says. "What is it that you don't want us to see? We're your friends. You can trust us." The firmness in her voice surprises Sam

The old Cassy, who was slowly being transformed over the past week, comes back in a rush. Shoulders hunched, looking down at her feet, she seems to shrink before Sam and Ally's eyes.

"Can't we just pretend that I live in a nice house, with a nice family like you guys do?" she mutters. "I don't *want* you to see who I really am." Her last words are barely audible, and Sam has to lean in close to hear her.

"Who you really are?" Sam repeats, her voice concerned. "I think I already know. That's why we're friends, Cassy. I see someone who is strong and brave. I'm proud to call you my friend. Nothing is going to change that."

Ally nods in agreement when Cassy looks back and forth between them. Could she trust them? Making up her mind, she puts one of her feet back on a pedal.

"Okay, but you have to swear that you won't tell *anyone* about it. Not even your parents." She makes the demand with an air of urgency, and again looks panic-stricken.

Sam is uncomfortable with the request. Unlike Lisa earlier, this is about more than spreading rumors at school. Cassy is asking her to keep a secret from her mom. While Sam often walks a fine line in sharing information, she never intentionally lies. Well, there was that one time that she and Hunter made a pact about the broken window on the back of the house. But they learned a painful lesson that day about things only getting worse if you fib. Plus, that was years ago. She isn't little anymore, and this could be important.

Cassy has started pedaling again, and she and Ally fall in behind her. Ally looks the same way that Sam is feeling. Raising her eyebrows at Sam, she shrugs before turning back to the road.

They follow Cassy down a nearly hidden driveway. There are rows of large cedar trees on either side of it, and their swooping branches reach out to meet in the middle. In some places, they have to duck to fit under the foliage. The asphalt is buried in cedar pines and broken branches, and it's evident that a car hasn't driven down this road in quite some time.

As they near the end, a small white house comes into view and Cassy turns back towards them. "Promise?" she asks again, wobbling a bit as she runs over a large branch.

Sam is trying to think of a way to make the promise that Cassy needs, without putting herself in a bad situation. She's saved from her dilemma by a shout from Ally.

"Is that smoke?"

Stopping, Sam looks to where Ally is pointing, and sure enough, there's a thin pillar of what looks like smoke.

"Grams!" Cassy cries, dropping the bike and sprinting towards the front door. "She must have tried to cook something!"

All three girls crash through the open front door, and are greeted by a horrible smell. Sam is so distracted by the fire, that she nearly overlooks the piles of stuff crammed into the foyer.

Following Cassy down the hall and into a long, narrow kitchen, the source of the smoke is clear. On the counter, flames are leaping out of a toaster, licking the underside of wooden cabinets above it.

"Grab some baking soda!" Sam screams, getting just close enough to pull the plug out of the wall.

Cassy throws open a couple of cupboards,

and quickly locates the box of soda. She understands why Sam asked for it, and rips the top open before dumping the contents on the fire. Thankfully, the baking soda smothers it almost instantly.

Grabbing a towel, Sam gingerly picks up the charred toaster, and Carries it out the back door, which Cassy is holding open. After setting it on the cement patio, they all gather around and stare down at what's sticking out of it.

"Grams must have put a cheese sandwich in it," Cassy explains, holding the burnt remains up gingerly. "She...gets confused about things. I should have never left her alone for so long! I made her food before I left yesterday, but I guess I didn't leave enough."

Dropping the ruined bread, she goes back inside, in search of her grandma. Sam and Ally follow without comment.

Now that the danger has passed, Sam takes in her surroundings. While the kitchen is mostly free of clutter, the rest of the house is packed. So much so, that they have to follow a narrow trail across the front room, foyer, and hallway. It's not so much garbage, but books, magazines, newspapers, loose papers, and boxes of all sorts and sizes. Mixed into it all are toys, clothes, and things that still have their price tags on them.

Ally reaches out and takes hold of Sam's hand. Sam looks back at her and sees that her friend is close to tears. Neither one of them can imagine what it must be like to live in a place like this. Sam has heard of hoarders, and watched a couple of shows about it, but this is first time she's been inside a house like this.

"Grams!" Cassy cries with relief. They've reached what must be the older woman's bedroom, and the only clean surface is a bed in the middle. Seated in the center of it is a small, graying woman in a bathrobe. She's sitting cross-legged with a plate on her lap and a half-eaten cheese sandwich. She apparently forgot that she even put another one in the toaster. She looks up at Cassy with dull eyes, but after a moment of confusion, they clear and then shine with recognition.

"Cassy!" she says happily. "You're home. Did you have a nice visit with your friends? Would you like a snack? I have a pie baking in the oven and the turkey dinner should be done soon."

Sam is shocked. There wasn't either a pie *or* a turkey cooking. The level of her grandma's deterioration is a lot more than Cassy was letting on.

"Thanks, Grams," Cassy says lovingly, patting her on the arm. "That sounds really good." Turning, she pulls a small cart closer to the bed. On it sits a compact television with a built-in CD player. Cassy pushes buttons and adjusts the volume until she is sure her grandma is happy, and then directs the girls out of the room. She doesn't even try to introduce them.

Crossing the hall, they go into the only other bedroom. It's like stepping into another house. Cassy's room is pristine. There is a small bed against the far wall, under a single window. An equally small dresser is to their left, and a desk to the right. Other than a few items on the desk, and her backpack on the bed, the room is bare.

"I like to keep it clean in here," she explains, closing the door behind them.

Sam is speechless for a moment, something that doesn't happen often. She simply doesn't know what to say. Crossing to the desk, she picks up a framed picture and studies it. In it is a young, very pretty lady with brown hair. Standing next to her holding her arm is a tall, handsome Hispanic man. "Are these your parents?" Sam asks.

Nodding, Cassy takes the photo and runs a finger across it. "Yes. They met in college, where they were both majoring in chemistry. Mom started late because she dropped out of high school when she was sixteen. Grams was proud of her, though, because she got her GED and then eventually a scholarship. They got married the summer after they graduated, and then she had me. That was when she was twenty-nine." Pausing, she blinks slowly and takes a breath.

"My mom died from cancer before I was one. Grams said that Dad loved her too much. He couldn't handle losing her, or the thought of raising a kid alone. He took off a few months later, so Grams has raised me ever since. She came back here to Oceanside with me when I was around two."

Setting the picture down, Cassy turns to the dresser and opens the bottom drawer. Taking out a box, she sets it on the bed, and the three girls sit around it. Once Cassy removes the lid, it's evident what it is: her box of memories.

"She loved me."

A binky, another picture of her as a baby being held by her mom, a lock of hair tied with a pink ribbon. Each item is placed carefully on the faded bedspread, the last one a newspaper clipping of her mom's obituary.

"Of course she loved you," Ally assures her, taking both of Cassy's hands in her own. "I'm sure your grandma loves you, too."

"She didn't use to be like this," Cassy says, pushing a family photo towards Ally. In it is a much younger version of her grandmother, standing with both of her parents at their wedding. "She was diagnosed with early dementia a little over three years ago. We did okay until last summer. I'll never forget the day we were driving home from the store, and she got lost. It flustered her so much, that she drove off the road and into a fence. When we got home, she parked the car behind the house, and has never driven again."

"Don't you have any other family?" Sam asks, looking at some papers lying in the bottom of the box. Picking the one off the top, she studies it absently.

"No. Grams and I have each other. We don't need anyone else."

"What about neighbors? Or the doctor? Hasn't anyone tried to…help you?" Ally presses.

"Grams was friends with one of the neighbors, who used to bring us dinner on Sundays and visit. But…she moved a couple of years ago to another state. The doctor's office stopped calling once the phone got disconnected. I couldn't figure out how to pay it," Cassy laughs lightly. "Grams gets social security and some other state program deposited automatically, and the mortgage and everything else comes out of it every month."

The document Sam is holding looks like a birth certificate. It has Cassy's mom's name on it, but the date doesn't look right. Setting it back in the bottom of the shoebox with some other legal-looking stuff, it seems insignificant at the moment. All Sam can think about is how Cassy is alone, trying to take care of her sick grandma. Looking up, Sam tries to figure out how to say what's on her mind, without upsetting her friend.

"She still has more good days than bad,"

Cassy adds quickly, seeing the look of concern on both Sam and Ally's faces. "She isn't normally the way she is tonight. It's just because I was gone, and it upset her. We walk together down to the store on the corner once a week for groceries, and Grams likes to cook dinner a couple of times a week. We play cards every evening and she normally tucks me in at night. We do okay."

"Cassy, *please* let me tell my mom," Sam pleads, not convinced. Cassy might think that they're doing okay, but Sam is afraid of what could happen if her grandma's condition gets any worse. "She can help you. I know she can!"

"No!" Cassy yells, scrambling backwards off the bed. "You can't! You can't tell *anyone!* They'll take her away, Sam. They'll put me in foster care and Grams in some mental facility. I'll never *see* her again! I'll never see *you* again! Please, Sam…Ally," she begs, crying now. "She's all I have!"

The raw fear on her friend's face is too much for Sam. Standing, she approaches Cassy and draws her into a big hug. Ally joins in, and the three of them stand that way for several minutes.

"I won't say anything, at least not for now,"

Sam whispers. "But I can't lie to my mom, so if she asks me about your home, I'll have to tell her the truth."

Cassy nods hesitantly, understanding that she can't demand that Sam lie for her.

"But you have to promise me," Sam adds, "that if things get any worse, you'll let us help you. Okay?"

"Okay," Cassy exhales, leaning her forehead against Sam's shoulder. "I promise."

13

RESTORATION

The following week, the girls work on the ranch every day after school. They get in a routine of riding the bus home, eating a snack, and then meeting on their bikes at the top of the hill. Cassy comes from the opposite direction, but the distance is almost the same. They end up having a couple of hours to pull weeds, rake, and trim trees.

Sam was afraid that she would have a hard time keeping her promise to Cassy, but fortunately, her mom hasn't pressed for information. She knows her mom suspects things aren't right, but she seems to be leaving it up to Sam to talk about it when she's ready.

John was more than happy to take the three of them to the outlet grocery store on Sunday. Ally came up with the idea, and Cassy wound up getting three times the food she could normally afford at the pricey gas station store near her home.

Sam and Ally discussed the whole situation at length and decided to do everything possible to help Cassy. But they'll have to turn to their parents if Grams gets any worse.

Sam's thoughts continue to drift back over the second week of school, as she pedals up the increasingly familiar steep road. Although it was better than the first week, she's still glad that it's Friday. The constant pressure is tiresome, both socially and mentally. It's been a struggle to keep up with the homework in addition to helping at the ranch, and her math is nearly impossible to understand. Thankfully, Hunter is better at it. The fact that she's willing to give her brother the whole "I'm smarter than you" ammunition is a testament to how desperate she is for help.

"How did you do on your math test?" Ally

huffs while standing on the pedals to get enough momentum.

"You must be reading my mind," Sam responds. "I think I at least passed. But if I want to ever do anything after school again in the near future, let's hope I got a C or better."

Grinning at each other, Sam and Ally ride the rest of the way in comfortable silence. As they approach the entrance to the ranch, they spot John's old bike leaning against the arch, but no sign of Cassy.

"Cassy!" Sam calls out, concerned when she doesn't hear an answer right away.

"Cassy!" Ally adds, her voice reflecting the same apprehension.

"I'm in here!" Cassy finally answers. "Come check out this trail I found!"

Sam and Ally abandon their bikes and follow the sound of Cassy's voice. They locate her on a barely recognizable pathway that leads off towards the back of the property.

"This is one of the trails that Ally and I always used to take," Sam explains, smiling at the memory. "It's been over a year, now, but it goes on forever."

"Doesn't this lead to some sort of monument?" Ally asks. She's pulling at the long grass growing over the trampled dirt, and breaking back obstructing branches.

"Yeah. There's a small lookout area part way down the hill," Sam tells Cassy. "Another trail leads to it from the opposite side. You know the city park by the library?" Sam asks, and Cassy nods. "Well, there used to be a trailhead marker there, but it hasn't been maintained since I don't know when. I think the lookout is a memorial or something that Mr. Covington paid for. At least, that's the name on the plaque there."

"We should work on clearing this trail after we're done around the house," Cassy suggests. "It would be cool to go hiking back in here!"

"What's the point?" Ally says. "Unless we can figure out a way to help Lisa keep the property, we won't be hiking on it."

The three of them fall silent, each lost in thought.

The stillness is interrupted by the distinct sound of a car pulling into the driveway. They often beat Lisa here, since she usually stays late to work on things in the classroom.

Emerging from the trail, they find Miss Covington looking at the three bikes. She smiles when she sees the girls. "There you are!" she calls happily through the open window. "Hurry up and meet me at the house. I have good news to share with you!"

The girls hurry up the driveway, eager to find out what has their teacher in such a good mood. Sam, of course, hopes Miss Covington has found a way to keep the estate.

"I just got done talking with the Hartfords," Lisa announces before the girls are even off their bikes. "They're another horse breeding family that my parents and I were close to. Their place is about fifty miles from here. I visit them when I can, because they've been watching over my most prized possession: Orion."

Sam is confused. What in the world is Lisa talking about?

"Who or what is Orion?" Ally is the first to ask.

"Orion is the last gift my father gave me, for my sixteenth birthday," Lisa tells them. "He's a magnificent Arabian horse. Dad purchased Orion from the Hartfords. When the estate fell apart and all the horses were being auctioned off, they offered to keep Orion for me so I wouldn't lose him. He's only thirteen, so not too old by horse standards, but definitely past his prime and not worth that much anymore. They've been talking about finding a retirement home for him, and have a potential buyer."

"That's so sad!" Ally cries, wondering how Lisa could be happy about it.

"No, Ally, it's not. Going to a good loving home in his later years is the best thing that could happen to Orion and I'm very thankful for it. What I'm most happy about right now, though, is that I might get to have him come stay here for a couple of months! The potential new owners are on the east coast, and can't collect him until after winter. If I can get one pasture and horse stall cleared out, I can bring him here."

"That's great!" Sam agrees, excited by the idea of possibly getting to help take care of a horse. She's had a decent amount of experience working with them.

"Sam knows an awful lot about horses," Ally tells Lisa. "We can help you!"

Lisa's smile broadens, and she looks younger

than usual. It dawns on Sam that Lisa *is* only twenty-five and recently out of college. Taking on a new job in addition to the task of selling her family's estate is a lot. She's glad to see her so happy.

"Well, we better get to work, then!" Sam tells Lisa, her smile just as big. "Because Orion is definitely going to come home!"

14

TRESSPASSING

They start work extra early Saturday morning. After Lisa showed them the far pasture Friday afternoon, it was clear that this would not be easy.

The three girls climb out of Lisa's car and begin gathering tools out of the trunk. Lisa navigated the older vehicle along the overgrown, gravel road with some difficulty, but managed not to get stuck. While it's a good trek from the house, it's the smallest fenced pasture with the best horse stall on it, so requires the least amount of work. Even then, the number of missing boards on the fence is high, and it will take all of them working together for several hours to clear the ground of debris. Sam knows how dangerous a large branch or rock can be to a running horse, and Lisa doesn't want to take any chance of Orion being injured.

The air is crisp, with a hint of fall that's just around the corner. It's not quite cold enough yet for a jacket, but the girls are glad they decided to wear their sweatshirts.

Sam picks up a crowbar and hammer, one in each hand. "What fence do you want me to demolish?" Sam asks, turning to Lisa. The plan is to go take boards off the fencing from the nearby fields, to use for repairs.

"Across that pasture," Lisa directs, pointing downhill. "It shares a fence with this one, so just grab whatever boards look good from the far side. First, why don't you and Ally walk the perimeter and count how many we need? I'm going to have Cassy help me clean the inside of the stall, and figure out what else needs to be done in there."

They spend the first half of the day just cleaning and collecting boards, and time flies by.

Sam only notices when it's lunchtime, because her stomach starts growling. Removing her gloves, she stands up tall and stretches her back. Prying the boards off is more difficult than she thought it would be.

"Ready to go take a break?" Lisa calls from the open door of the horse stall.

Ally drops the board Sam just handed her, and waves back in confirmation. "Coming!" she hollers, happy at the thought of getting to sit for a while.

"I can make us some sandwiches," Lisa offers when they all meet back at her car. "If you don't mind," she continues, "I'd like to walk back. I don't want to drive on this road more than I have to, until the new gravel is delivered. I didn't realize how bad it would be. I'll leave it here for now, though, so we can use it to haul back the gear later."

As they all begin to cut across the fields, Sam breaks out in a run. "I've had to use the bathroom for the last two hours!" she shouts over her shoulder. "I'll see you there!"

"I don't know how she can possibly run," Cassy laughs, shaking her head. "Does she *ever* run out of energy?"

"I haven't seen it happen yet," Ally replies, linking her arm in Cassy's.

It takes Sam less than five minutes to reach the more manicured lawn of the house, and is surprised to see an unfamiliar car in the driveway.

It has be Lisa's aunt, Clara Wells, Sam figures, jumping the front steps two at a time. Lisa told them earlier that her aunt was going to stop by later for a visit. She must have come earlier than expected.

The front door is ajar, which Sam doesn't give much thought to. Mrs. Wells *does* own the house, so it would only be natural for her to let herself in. But as Sam crosses the foyer, and starts down the hallway, a large crashing sound comes from the nearby office.

"Hello?" she calls, headed in that direction. "Mrs. Wells? Are you okay?"

Sam is answered by an even louder thud, and the distinct sound of a heavy chair being pushed across the maple floor.

What in the world? She thinks, running now. While someone else might choose to run *away* from the confusing situation, Sam's instinct is to go towards it, still thinking that Mrs. Wells must need help.

As Sam approaches the doorway, a large figure suddenly races forward. It's definitely *not* Mrs. Wells. Throwing her hands up in alarm, Sam tries to dodge out of the man's way, but isn't fast enough. He slams into her in his rush to leave. While trying to catch her balance, she grabs at him and latches onto something he's got sheltered in his arms. The object comes loose as she bounces off his solid form and crashes into the wall behind her.

As Sam's breath is nearly knocked from her lungs, she looks up and gasps in shock at Peter Covington's stunned face. He stumbles back a step before recovering his footing, and then glares at Sam, his grey eyes narrowing. They both look down at what Sam now recognizes as Lisa's computer case, lying on the floor between them.

"What are you doing?" Sam demands, her voice wavering. It seems clear that he was attempting to leave with the laptop, but she's not quite ready to call him a thief.

The older man tips his head to the side in a contemplative gesture, studying her face. When he finally speaks, his voice is low and dangerous.

"That isn't a question you have a right to ask, young lady. Now, step aside so I can go speak with my niece." His last words are almost drowned out by the pounding sound of several people on the front porch. His head jerks up in response, his brow furrowing even further.

Too angry to be as scared as she should be, Sam reaches out and picks up the laptop case before he has a chance to, and then steps aside, giving him plenty of room to pass by.

Hesitating for a tense moment, Peter Covington huffs loudly and stalks past her. Sam hears him call out a greeting to Lisa, as if it were a perfectly normal thing for him to be inside her home.

15

AUNT CLARA

"Uncle Peter!" Sam hears Lisa shout from the front door, as she runs to catch up. "What are you doing in my house? I told you that you can't be here!"

Sam goes to stand in between Ally and Cassy as Peter approaches Lisa, who is still out in the driveway. The three girls exchange a look, unsure if they should get involved.

The bright, early afternoon light fades as the sun slips behind a cloud, darkening the features of the man's face.

"I came to try and speak with you again," he

states, jamming his hands in the pockets of his charcoal-colored slacks. "We're family, Lisa. Can't we even talk?"

Lisa looks at him questioningly, and it's obvious that she's thrown off by the comment. "What is there to talk about? You weren't interested in discussing anything the other day. Demanding to be let inside and then threatening me when I said no, isn't exactly a great way to start a conversation."

Dropping his head slightly, Peter nods in agreement. "You're right, dear. I owe you an apology. I went about things the wrong way. All I want to do is collect some old photographs from your father's office. I've been working on putting together some information on our Covington name. When I got here and didn't see your car, I thought you were gone and let myself in when I found the door unlocked. I was going to leave you a note."

"Then what were you doing with *this*?" Sam asks, holding out the black leather case. She doesn't believe him, and hopes that Lisa isn't falling for it.

Lisa's expression changes and she stares at

her uncle accusingly. "You had my laptop?"

"Don't be ridiculous," he states, his tone changing. "I was simply moving it from the desk, when Sam came in and surprised me. Now, can we go in and talk?"

Lisa looks uncomfortable, and glances up at the house, at her uncle, and then the driveway. "We can't," she finally says, fidgeting nervously. "Aunt Clara could be here any minute. This isn't my house, Uncle Peter, and we need to honor the fact that she doesn't want you here. Maybe we can meet somewhere for coffee, and you can explain what you're looking --"

Before Lisa can finish the invitation, Peter cuts her off by throwing his arms up dramatically in the air. "Never mind!" he shouts, stomping towards his car. "I thought we could be civil with each other, but I see that isn't going to work. So be it."

Lisa stands with her mouth open, unsure how to respond. Her eyes fill with tears as he slams his door and then drives recklessly around the fountain before speeding up the drive.

"I'm sorry," Sam says, feeling horrible for her.

"It's not your fault," Lisa replies, wiping at her eyes. Straightening, she pushes the hair back from her face and takes a deep breath. "I'm sorry if he scared you. Did he bother you at all?"

"No," Sam tells her, not wanting to cause her any further grief. "I was just surprised, that's all. But he *was* walking out of the office with the computer."

Laughing, Lisa takes the laptop in question. "Sam, my uncle is a lot of things, but he certainly isn't a thief. He's got millions. What would he want with this old thing?"

"Maybe it wasn't so much the computer, but what's on it?" Cassy suggests. They all turn to look at Cassy, and the smile fades from Lisa's face.

"Do you think he's serious about trying to blame me for stealing the gem? Maybe he thinks he can find something incriminating in my documents or emails." Lisa looks pale and starts wringing her hands. "Of course, he wouldn't find anything. But the thought is still unsettling."

Just then, the sound of another car reaches them, and they all jump, afraid that Peter Covington has returned.

"It's my Aunt Clara!" Lisa explains, breathing a sigh of relief. Running up to a large, red truck, she opens the door and then embraces a grey-haired woman after she climbs down. They stand talking quietly for a minute, heads close. The woman is shorter than Lisa is, hardly even five feet tall. Although thin, she has a strong presence about her and it's clear to the girls that Lisa is relieved to have her there.

Clara leads her niece up to the house, patting her comfortingly on the arm. "You've got to be Sam," she says pleasantly, pausing in front of the girls. "Lisa has told me quite a bit about you. And you have to be Ally, the girl with red hair," she continues lightly, before Sam has a chance to answer.

"And this is their friend, Cassy," Lisa explains. "They've all been a great help to me this past week."

"Let's all go inside," Clara suggests. "We can have some lunch and talk about ... well, discuss what's best in regards to Peter.

They all gather in the den, which faces the front of the property. It's a warm, comforting room with wood-paneled walls and a river rock fireplace. Taking a seat in between Cassy and Ally on a large, leather sofa, Sam finally starts to relax.

"Aunt Clara, I know you're upset that Uncle Peter was here, but I'd really rather not call the police. I don't think they'd charge him with trespassing, since his last name *is* Covington."

Clara chooses to stand, running her hand along the edge of a built-in bookcase, and then wiping the dust off on her jeans. While her face is pleasant, her eyes are dark and piercing, and her back is rigid. "I agree that it's best to keep this in the family."

Lisa appears surprised by this announcement, tilting hear head at her aunt. "Really, Aunt Clara? I thought you'd be more concerned about him being in the house."

Shaking her head, her shoulders sag a bit and she leans against a table. "Lisa, that man went through every inch of this house with me the week after your parents died. I can't imagine what it is that he hopes to find."

"He said he wanted family photos," Ally offers.

Snorting now, Clara turns to Lisa. "Photos? Really? What *is* that man up to?"

"He had my laptop, and I'm worried that he might be serious about implicating me in the Eye of Orion theft." Lisa looks close to tears again, but Clara is non-pulsed.

"That's ridiculous! The police already cleared you, and what does he care? He got the insurance money. Granted, it was an outdated policy so not what the gem is worth today, but it was still an incredible sum."

"It's been three years since the ruby was taken. Why harass me about it now?" Lisa wonders, plopping down in a chair.

"The only thing that's changed is that you're back in the house," Sam concludes. "You've caught him snooping around here twice now since then, going through your things. He's got to be looking for something."

Clara turns to study Sam, who squirms a little under her scrutiny. Clara's stare is intense, but after a moment, she slowly closes her eyes and takes a huge, raspy breath. When her eyes open again, they've changed, and it's clear that she's made up her mind about something. Going to the matching chair across from Lisa, she sits down, and then reaches out to grasp Lisa's hands.

"I think it's time I told you what happened between Peter and me," Clara says.

16

A FAMILY DIVIDED

Pausing, Aunt Clara glances at the three young girls on the couch, and then back at Lisa.

"Oh, they can stay," Lisa tells her aunt. "Unless it's something they shouldn't hear."

Shaking her head, Clara waves a hand. "It's nothing scandalous, just the age-old fight of money. When my sister first married your dad," Clara tells Lisa, "I saw Peter quite often. He was at every major family gathering. While the brothers weren't terribly close, they got along. That all changed after your grandfather died. It was dreadful. Peter at least went to the funeral, but stood at the fringes of the cemetery and didn't bother to go support his mother at the reception afterward. He was rather absent from the whole process, and I don't think your dad ever forgave him for that."

"What happened with The Eye of Orion?" Sam asks hesitantly. "Why did they fight over it?"

"To explain, I need to give you the background on the ruby," Clara says, more open about it than Sam had hoped she would be. "Samuel Covington, Lisa's Grandpa, was an interesting man. He was a magnificent architect and traveled the world, designing homes and buildings. When he was in Burma, he bought The Eye of Orion for around twenty-five thousand dollars. He used his own inheritance from his father's passing earlier that year. He apparently wanted to invest it in something beautiful to be handed down through the generations. That isn't a huge sum of money, even back then, but enough to make it valuable. And it *was* magnificent! I saw it once, when I went to have Christmas supper at their home one year. Even though it was worth more than their whole estate by then, it was simply nestled in a wooden box, lined in silk. I'll never forget how the ruby reflected the firelight back, so that it looked like a star was trapped inside it!

"You see, Samuel didn't care about how much it was worth. Actually, he was never impressed with money and wealth. His oldest son, Jack, felt the same way, but his youngest son, Peter, was much greedier. Jack, Lisa's dad," she directs to Sam, "went out of his way to avoid getting caught up in anything monetary. When he received his inheritance, he immediately invested it into the horses. He could have bought a much nicer house somewhere, but this ranch was his dream.

"Peter put his share into the stock market, which helped launch his career as an investor. In spite of that wealth, he was still unhappy, since the ruby was worth ten times as much, and he believed they should sell it.

"Jack was very tight-lipped about it, but Samuel's widow and I had a whispered conversation a couple of years later, right before her passing. Apparently, while on his deathbed, Samuel told his sons that his wish was for the ruby to be passed on to their own children, and not sold. It was never meant as a prize, but rather a rare charm, and to mark their unity as a family. When the brothers got into a heated argument, Samuel asked his wife to leave and closed the door behind her. When Peter and Jack emerged some time later, it was never spoken of out in the open again. The ruby was gone, and Samuel didn't write its disposition into his will."

"When I was younger, I tried to get dad to talk to me about it," Lisa remembers. "But he would just smile, rub the top of my head, and tell me that one day I would get to see it. I gave up asking when I was about twelve. The family 'story' was that Grandpa gave the ruby to Peter, and the authentication paperwork to Dad. This would prevent it from being sold, but still keep the brothers connected, whether they liked it or not."

"Yes, that's what I always believed, too," Clara confirms. "Peter was at their funeral, but we didn't speak to one another. Of course, he was sure to be present at the reading of the will, hovering like a vulture. He was infuriated when the estate and bank holdings were given to me, even though the amount of cash was small in comparison to what he makes.

"The money was all tied up in the horses, and since Jack and Melissa were unconcerned about extravagant wealth, they never kept much in the bank. They weren't even on top of their will. It was years old, and quite inadequate. I didn't even think to question why it didn't mention the ruby, since I always assumed Peter already had it. The one thing they were careful about, though, was making sure Lisa was taken care of. That's why they *did* invest in substantial life insurance, making her the beneficiary. While the estate was left to me, it was with clear instructions to be used for raising Lisa."

"The horses were worth more than the property," Lisa breaks in, her eyes dreamy as she recalls the animals. "Some of the most sought after breeding horses in the country. We also had a top-notch trainer that people came from all over to work with."

"Yes," Clara says, frowning. "Michael Stuart. He worked at Covington Ranch for nearly ten years, and was a trusted employee and friend. Jack left his prized horse to him. We all assumed Michael would take over managing the ranch after the accident. Instead, less than a month after he found out that the prized horse was his, the scoundrel left and took several of our other employees with him, to start his own business. I was at a total loss in the aftermath, without a *clue* of how to run things. A couple of the other ranch hands tried to help, but we were quickly in the red. By the end of the first year, I realized I had to sell the remaining horses and close it down, or risk losing everything."

Sam and Ally look at each other, saddened to hear the story behind the property they've enjoyed over the years.

"After the will was read that day, Peter approached me," Lisa continues. "He was upset, and asked what was to be done about the ruby. I had just buried my sister and her husband, and the only thing the man cared about was the ruby! I was angry. I told him I didn't care what he did with it.

"He seemed taken aback by this, and after a moment of confusion, his whole demeanor changed. I assumed at the time that it was because he realized how callous he was being. He asked if I needed any help in going through the estate, and settling things. To be honest with you, I was overwhelmed, consumed with grief, and terrified to raise a sixteen year old on my own. The thought of having help was a relief, and Peter w*as* Jack's only close remaining family, as I was Melissa's. So I welcomed his assistance.

"At first, he was like the answer to my prayers. He helped set up a way to organize, document, and fairly disperse anything of value. We spent a whole week going through each room methodically. On the sixth day, he came to me one evening with a picture frame in his hands. It was The Eye of Orion certification from the wall of Jack's den. In order to have the ruby insured, it went through a very thorough inspection and appraisal process. It was nearly worthless without the document. He asked if he could take it, and I didn't even hesitate to say yes. The family squabble over a ruby was the least of my worries. The papers meant nothing to me and held no value on their own. I had the estate and I still thought that Lisa had a fortune coming to her from the life insurance.

"The next day, Peter didn't show up to help. It also happened to be the day that I received notice from the insurance company that they were launching an investigation. They were questioning whether Lisa was a legal heir. After meeting with Jack and Melissa's attorney, it turned out that he was never given Lisa's birth certificate, or her adoption paperwork. It was a nightmare. I was the only person that knew of the adoption, Peter didn't even know. That's how little he saw his brother. It was a closed adoption and Lisa was three when they built the ranch, so no one else in the area ever questioned if she was their biological daughter.

"I couldn't believe they hadn't shared this vital information with their attorney. I know that they couldn't possibly have contemplated a future where they would both be taken from Lisa's life at the same time. They must have relied on the surviving parent to bring forth the required paperwork ... but," Clara pauses, wiping at her eyes. "Anyway, we couldn't find it. Not anywhere. No birth certificate, no adoption documents, no records of a safe deposit box somewhere. I was frantic. I hired a private investigator and spent countless sleepless nights pouring through every box in the attic and basement."

"That reminds me, Lisa," Clara adds. "It's your twenty-sixth birthday next Sunday!"

"Yes, and if everything goes well," Lisa tells her aunt, "I should have Orion delivered on Saturday. The perfect birthday gift!"

"I'm so grateful that the Hartfords took Orion," Clara answers, her smile fading. "At least he was spared the chaos in the end. When Michael left with our most famous horse, I knew we were in real trouble. I went to Peter and begged him to sell the ruby, and give half of the money to Lisa. While I knew it went against what Jack originally wanted, I felt sure that taking care of his daughter would be the most important thing to him. Peter actually *laughed* at me! He said that even if he did decide to sell, since Lisa couldn't prove she was a Covington, he had no legal obligation to share any of the funds with her. He closed the door in my face.

"My attorney regrettably agreed with the assessment. Since it wasn't in the will, the ruby couldn't be claimed by either of us. If it was already part of the estate, we could try and fight it that way, but since it was never in our possession, we have no right to it."

"What a horrible thing to do!" Ally gasps, totally caught up in the story.

"He had the nerve to come to me three years later, offering to buy the house," Clara says, nodding in agreement with Ally's comment. "Even though it would have been a relief to not have the responsibility, I was too mad at the man to consider it. Three years after that, he made another bid that was twice as much as the house was worth. I have to admit I was tempted. By then, four years ago, I knew that I was eventually going to be forced to sell it. But I still refused. Lisa was just starting college then and doing well. My plan was always to turn the house over to her, once she was financially set and able to make her own decision as to whether to keep it or not."

"What if he never had the ruby?" Sam suddenly asks. Everyone looks surprised, except for Clara.

"I suspected that," Clara tells Sam, "After he made the first offer on the house. I never saw him with The Eye of Orion, and he didn't sell it. But then why go through the whole charade to take the certification?"

"So that he could sell the ruby if he managed to find it," Lisa answers. "Or, use it to collect the insurance on the *fake* ruby he arranged to have stolen!" Groaning, Lisa lowers her head and covers her face with her hands. "Not only was I set up by John Brown," she murmurs in between her fingers, "But I was used by my own uncle!"

"So you think that when he couldn't find the real ruby, he had a fake made? Then he hired that guy to use Lisa as a way to make the insurance company believe it was the real one?" Cassy surmises, putting it all together.

"Yes," Sam confirms. "Lisa was the perfect witness."

"And it worked," Lisa says sadly, looking up. "Now, he must be worried that I might find the real Eye of Orion here somewhere, and expose him for the fraud he really is. He'd go to jail for years."

"But it's not here," Clara says with confidence. "I've been through the whole house several times, looking for your birth certificate. He doesn't have anything to worry about. Your grandpa could have even kept the darn thing, and had it buried with him, for all we know!"

"Maybe," Sam says slowly, looking at each of them in turn. "But if it's here, we've got to find it!"

17

CHANGES

Sunday morning begins like a postcard for early fall, with a bright blue sky lending little warmth to the ground, which is now becoming littered with dropped leaves.

Sam's tires crunch through them, and she turns her face up to the sunshine, closing her eyes briefly. She knows this road well enough to trust that her bike will stay on course. She'll often glide down a hill with her eyes shut and arms spread out wide, pretending she's flying.

Ally and Cassy laugh about something behind her, and she looks back for a moment, to make sure she isn't getting too far ahead. While she'd rather be up at Covington Ranch, searching out a possible location for The Eye of Orion, she's happy to be with her friends.

Not wanting to involve the girls any further in her family problems, Lisa had immediately shut down any chance of a treasure hunt. She had even called Sam's mom, explaining the uncomfortable situation with her uncle. Kathy was understanding, and said she didn't have a problem with Sam still helping out with yardwork. But she did warn Sam to keep her nose clean.

Lisa insisted that they take today off. Turns out it's for the best, because Cassy asked her and Ally to go somewhere with her that's very special. It's the anniversary of Cassy's mom's death. Eleven years ago today, cancer took her away, and ever since she was old enough, she's gone to put flowers on her mother's grave.

Pulling into the parking lot of the one city park their town maintains, Sam feels a sudden, sharp sense of loss for Cassy. It makes her appreciate her mom, and feel a bit guilty about how she felt last night during the light lecture she received. Sam can't begin to imagine what it would be like, not having her mom around.

"Thanks for doing this, you guys," Cassy says, dropping her bike in the grass. "I've never come to the cemetery by myself. Grams has always been with me, but when I mentioned it yesterday, she got very upset and was off for the rest of the day. I think it's too much for her now. She was doing okay this morning, and I was afraid to upset her again."

"We're honored to come with you," Ally replies, looping an arm through Cassy's.

Sam goes to Cassy's other side, and together, the three of them head up a gravel trail. It parallels an older, unmaintained path for a short distance, and Sam realizes that it's the one she was telling Cassy about the other day, the trail that leads to the Covington memorial.

They soon turn in the other direction, towards an ornate stone entrance, while the other route heads up the hill and into the woods.

Sam has never been in the town's cemetery before, and she's nervous. Crossing the threshold, she sees that it's a large space, spotted with mature maple trees and surrounded by a high, wrought-iron fence. The footpath branches out into orderly rows, which then thread in between the various headstones. Other than a couple of angel statues, small, plain square cement plaques dominate the cemetery.

Cassy heads towards the back right corner, and Sam and Ally follow silently. Other than one other person lingering on the opposite side, they're alone. The cemetery has the same feeling as a church, inspiring whispers and hushed tones. The girls are careful to be respectful. Sam pauses every now and then to read the cement squares. She's amazed at the various dates and names, and can't help but wonder about the people they represent.

Scattered among the nondescript headstones are larger, more elaborate carvings. Cassy stops in front of one of the bigger ones, under a shady tree, and Sam catches her breath when she sees the name 'Sanchez' etched into the top. It's about four by three feet, and a good twelve inches thick. It's made of a beautiful white marble, with glittering veins of silver threaded through it. Under the proper name is the first name of Elizabeth, her date of birth and death, and then a carving of horseshoe, below. It had to have cost a fortune.

"What a stunning tombstone," Ally whispers.

"Grams told me it was anonymously donated a few years after she was buried," Cassy explains, kneeling to place her small bouquet of flowers at its base. "I like to think it was from my dad."

"I'm sure it was," Ally agrees. "I'm sure he loves you, too, Cassy."

Cassy shrugs and then sits quietly in the grass to the side of the grave.

"Have you ever thought of trying to find him?" Sam asks. She's hesitant to bring it up, but if Cassy's grandma is getting worse, she might need to explore all of her options.

"No!" Cassy says with some anger, shaking her head vigorously. "He's known were I'm at. Mom grew up in this town, but she and Grams moved when she was sixteen. They had always planned on coming back. That's why Grams had her buried here, and then moved here with me. She said they still considered it home.

"No," Cassy repeats, standing now and wiping her hands off on her jeans. "I don't have a father anymore. All I have is Grams."

****

The pounding on the door sounds frantic, and Sam knows immediately that something is wrong.

She's sitting at the dinner table with her mom, Hunter, and the twins, having their customary Sunday night super. She just got through telling them about the earlier trip to the cemetery.

Sam is the first to spring up from her chair, and beats Hunter to the door. Pulling it open, she's shocked to see Cassy, her face stricken and eyes red from crying.

"It's Grams," Cassy chokes out, before Sam can ask what's wrong. "She finally asked me where I was today, and when I told her … she got upset again. But this time," she continues, fresh tears spilling over, "She forgot who I was, Sam! Grams started *yelling* at me to get out of her house, like I was a burglar or something. When I tried to calm her down, she grabbed my arm, and tried to *drag* me out! I've never seen her like this. I don't know what to do!" Sobbing now, Cassy covers her face with her hands.

Hunter just stares back and forth between Cassy and his sister, at a total loss, but Sam doesn't hesitate. Gently, she takes Cassy by the shoulders, guiding her inside, and takes her straight to her mom.

Sam does most of the talking, with Cassy simply nodding and adding information only when necessary. Kathy is kind, but doesn't give any choices as to what has to be done. She calls 911, requesting a welfare check at the address, after explaining that she believes the elderly woman is suffering from dementia or Alzheimer's and might not be safe.

It's a tense, long forty-five minutes before an officer calls back. Kathy speaks with him in muted tones from the kitchen. Sam and Cassy sit in the family room with the television on. They aren't really paying attention to it though, and it's just a distraction.

Finally, Sam's mom comes in and sits across from them, silencing the game show. "Your grandma is okay, Cassy," she reassures the scared girl. "But she needs medical care. The officer said that the hospital is just starting to run some tests, but it's already obvious that they'll be admitting her and holding her for at least a few days, while they determine what's going to be the best thing for her."

"They're going to take her away!" Cassy wails, panic-stricken.

"Cassy," Kathy says soothingly, leaning forward. "I know you love your grandma very much, and you want what's best for her, right?" When Cassy nods, she takes one of her hands. "You know that she hasn't been well. With Alzheimer's, it becomes very hard, and then impossible for family members to care for their loved ones. You have nothing to be ashamed of. They're going to take very good care of your grandma."

"I know she needs help," Cassy confirms, wiping back tears and visibly working to calm herself down. "I just don't want them to put her in a home, and then make me go to a foster family where I can never see her again!" The thought threatens to bring on a round of fresh tears, but Kathy cuts her off.

"I talked to the officer about that. Child Protective Services *will* have to get involved at some point, if they determine that she can't go back home. But, I assured the officer that you are more than welcome to stay here with us, until it can be worked out. The policeman is old friends with Sam's dad, and knows our family well. He said he's fine with letting you remain here for now."

To Sam's surprise, Cassy suddenly throws herself forward into Kathy's arms, wrapping her up in a big hug. Kathy gently pats the girl's back, and looks at Sam over the top of Cassy's head.

Yeah, Sam thinks, fighting back her own tears now. *I don't know what I'd do without my mom.*

18

ORION LANDING

In spite of the traumatic experience Sunday night, the next week flies by in a flurry of fun activities. There is a sense of excitement over the pending arrival of Lisa's horse, and the field and stall go from unusable to acceptable in a matter of days.

Cassy is allowed to visit her grandma on Tuesday, right after school. Sam's mom takes her, but Sam and Ally wait in the car, to give her privacy. To their surprise, she's smiling when she returns. The hospital is going to keep her grandma for up to another week, due to some ongoing health concerns, but she's better than

Cassy has seen her in more than a year. Cassy finally understands that her grandma needs more care than she can provide and will be much better off in a facility where she can get it.

Cassy fits right into the Wolf household. Although space is tight, there is so much warmth and love, that Cassy is the happiest she can ever remember being. Aside from missing her grandma, and being anxious about what will happen when the week is up, she's never felt so safe and content.

On Wednesday, Sam approaches her mom about letting Cassy live with them. They all like the idea, even Hunter. But Kathy explains that it just doesn't work that way with the state. There is a process in place. Once any chance of a family member caring for Cassy is ruled out, then they begin the placement procedure. To be considered as a foster family involves a complicated series of requirements and interviews. It doesn't happen quickly, and Cassy likely won't be allowed to stay with them until they are accepted. Once her grandma is officially judged as unable to care for her, and put into an adult home, Cassy will probably be taken as a ward of the state.

While the kids are discouraged by the news, Cassy remains hopeful, since Kathy promises to speak with Sam's dad about it. If he agrees, she's going to talk with Family Services, and apply for custody.

When Saturday rolls around, thoughts of mean uncles and stolen gems have faded to the back of Sam's mind. She's been so busy with homework, yardwork, Cassy, and dreams of riding Orion, that it simply doesn't seem that important anymore.

It's a bright and unseasonably warm morning when the group of five kids crests the hill to Covington Ranch. John and Hunter have a rare, practice-free Saturday. They've offered to spend it working on the broken fountain. John wanted to drive everyone to the house, but the girls are so used to the trek now that they enjoy it. Plus, being on bikes gives the guys the advantage of leaving whenever they want, without having to worry about how the girls will get home.

"Wait until you see the place," Ally chirps, her legs pumping hard to keep up with the bigger boys.

"I've been up there tons of times," Hunter

answers. "John and I would take our airsoft guns and have shootouts."

"Man, that was like, what? I think three or four years ago. Seems like forever," John reminisces. He and Hunter drifted apart the last couple of years, after John started high school, leaving his younger friend back in middle school. But now, after a fun summer trip together, they're back on the same campus, and as close as ever.

Sam glances over at Ally's older brother, noting the bright sparkle the dappled sunlight causes in his vibrant blue eyes. His blonde hair is a far cry from Ally's bright red, and he's much taller. He's also a whole lot nicer than her own brother is, even though she and Hunter don't fight as much as they used to.

"Slowpoke!" Hunter shouts as he suddenly speeds past her and smacks her lightly on the back of the head, dispelling any pleasant thoughts she had of him.

Cassy laughs at their antics as Sam struggles to catch up and return the tag. But it turns out that Hunter's daily football practice proves more strengthening than Sam's bike rides and he pulls ahead.

"Come on, guys!" Ally hollers, sweating now as she pushes even harder. "This isn't a race." She's beginning to regret not taking John up on his offer to drive.

Ally and Cassy are just catching up to Sam and the boys as they reach the driveway to the ranch. Ally stares up at the large, metal letters hanging above them while she pedals under. The letters have more meaning for her now, since she actually knows a Covington.

Lisa is waiting for them, anxiously bouncing on the heels of her feet. Her smile is contagious, and any thoughts of sibling rivalry or tiring biking are quickly forgotten. Today is the day that Orion gets to come home!

"Lisa, this is my brother, Hunter, and Ally's brother, John," Sam states, introducing the teens to her teacher.

She shakes each of their hands, surprising them with the strength of her grip. Lisa was brought up to believe that a limp handshake was a sign of someone who was insecure ... or insincere.

"Welcome! Thanks for coming, you guys. I

don't know if this old, crumbly thing can be salvaged," Lisa explains, waving a glove at the broken fountain and pond spread around it. "I haven't even tried to turn it on. I'm afraid it'll just flood everything."

"I helped my dad put our underground sprinkler system in," Hunter explains, "So I know a little about the piping and stuff. I might be able to figure it out."

"And my scout group built a pond last summer for an older couple," John tells her, ignoring Hunter's eye-rolling. John's skills picked up through his membership are a source of many jokes, but it's all good-natured.

"Well, if you can do something with it, I'll be very impressed! All of the tools and supplies I have are in the small shed here next to the house. If something you need isn't there, just let me know. Now," Lisa continues, turning to Sam and the other two girls. "I had some fresh hay delivered this morning, and there are pitchforks in the largest barn, out around back. Who wants to help spread it before Orion gets here?"

The three of them race off, leaving Lisa laughing behind them. Sam beats Ally and Cassy, but she's so winded when she gets there, that she fails to pick up a pitchfork. Cassy grabs one, but then turns and hands it to Sam.

"How about we take turns?" she suggests, tilting her head to the side in much the same manner that Lisa does when she's considering something.

Less than an hour later, the last of the hay has just been spread out in the stall. The timing is perfect, as the hum and clang of a large truck pulling a trailer rumbles up the rough dirt lane.

"Orion!" Lisa cries, dropping her rake and running outside.

After greeting the driver, an older man with iron-colored hair and a worn cowboy hat, Lisa hurries to the back of the trailer. Although it's been nearly nine years since she worked the ranch, she opens the latches with a practiced grace, and leaps inside.

Sam watches eagerly, and then catches her breath when Lisa leads out the most magnificent horse she has ever seen. He's tall, close to twenty hands, and the color of midnight. His muscles ripple under his satin coat, which shines with a heavenly brilliance in the sunlight. His mane hangs long and loose, and he tosses it at the girls, as if he knows how handsome he is.

As soon as he's on solid ground, Lisa wraps her arms around his neck. After a brief moment where it seems like he is going to try and pull away, he freezes, his muscles visibly tensing. Snickering, he then turns his head, burying his nose into Lisa's neck, his nostrils flaring as he breathes in her scent. She murmurs something close to his ear, and with a flick of his tail, the horse is transformed. He shudders, whinnies and begins lifting his front feet rhythmically, all the while nibbling at Lisa's neck, chin, and finally her hair.

"He remembers you!" Ally squeals, clapping her hands happily.

"Horses have an incredible memory," the man, who must be Mr. Hartford, explains, coming around the trailer. "He knows exactly who Lisa is."

Lisa finally breaks away from her old friend, eyes misty, and talks with Mr. Hartford briefly before he leaves. Once the back of the trailer is out of sight, she turns back to Orion.

"Sam, would you like to meet him?" she asks,

holding onto his lead.

Walking up to the Arabian, careful to stay where he can see her, so as not to spook him, Sam reaches out a hand, palm up, for him to smell. When he appears satisfied with her scent, she moves on to touch his neck, shoulders, and then his back, slowly gaining the horse's trust.

As she runs a hand along his flank, she notices a unique brand on his haunches. Unlike the standard C/R hooked together, this one is more intricate. The C is turned sideways, with several lines dissecting it, and what looks like a star in the center.

"Why is this brand different?" Sam asks, turning to face Lisa.

"Dad had one specially made for Orion, since he was my horse and not a part of the ranch stock. It was just another way for him to make Jupe special for me."

Sam smiles at the nickname, and then turns back to her new friend. Orion won't be here for long, but she hopes that his visit helps Lisa find some peace. Her smile falters slightly at the realization that *Lisa* won't be here much longer, either. Glancing at the special brand again, created by a loving father who is now gone, Sam's desire to make things right at the ranch is rekindled. Her only fear is that they're running out of time.

19

DECEPTIONS

It's been a long day. Sam watches silently as Hunter and John battle out an intense game of foosball, smack-talking each other as their little wooden men kick a soccer ball back and forth. She nibbles absent-mindedly at a large piece of pizza, distracted by her own thoughts of horses, gems, and lost parents.

"When do you think we'll be able to ride Orion?" Cassy asks, looking at both Sam and Ally for an answer.

The three of them are gathered around a folding table at the far end of the game room in

Ally and John's house. Sam was surprised by the invitation for a sleepover. Ally's parents, Brandon and Elizabeth Parker, don't normally like a lot of activity going on when they're trying to relax during their rare time off from work together. However, they are both sitting on the couch at the other end, watching an intense football game on the big screen TV.

According to John, one of the teams playing is from the college his dad went to, and briefly played ball for, until a knee injury took him out. Mr. Parker shouts good-naturedly at the television, before throwing popcorn towards it.

"It's going to be a while before Orion is settled enough," Sam replies, finishing her pizza and finding a napkin to wipe her fingers on. "Lisa said at least a couple of days. I don't blame her, either, he's a big horse!"

Picking up a pencil, Sam starts doodling Orion's brand on her napkin. She can't seem to get the custom design out of her head.

"What's that?" Startled by the voice near her ear, Sam jumps and then laughs at herself when she finds John looking over her shoulder.

"It's just the brand on Orion. Pretty cool,

huh?"

"But I thought the Covington mark was a C and R hooked together?" Hunter asks, joining the rest of them around the table.

"It is," Ally offers. "But Lisa's dad had one designed just for Orion, because he was a gift to Lisa."

Shrugging, Hunter picks up two huge pieces of pizza, one in each hand. Grinning, he stacks them together and then takes a big bite. Not to be outdone, Cassy does the same and they're soon in a race to see who can finish first.

"That's pretty disgusting," Ally mutters, scooting back out of the way when a chunk of peperoni comes flying at her.

"Hmmm." Ignoring the food challenge, John picks up the napkin and studies the image. Turning it first one way, and then the other, he takes it with him over to his laptop that's charging on a side table.

Intrigued, Sam and Ally follow him, sitting to either side on a small loveseat. Sam figures out what he's doing as soon as he opens a map program. Entering the address for Covington Ranch, he selects a topographical version, and then pivots it around back and forth a few times.

"There!" both he and Sam say at the same time.

"What?" Ally asks, totally lost. "I don't get it."

"If this were to represent the top of the hill, where the house is," John explains, pointing to the crest of the C. "Then this could be the trail leading down past the memorial," he continues, tracing the first horizontal line.

"Isn't there a creek that runs past the memorial?" Ally questions, starting to see it, too.

"Yeah, there is!" Sam gasps, pointing to the other, thicker line that matches up with the creek. "I remember talking about trying to fish in it for trout one summer."

"This final line would be the one that goes past the memorial and ends up at the city park," John concludes. "It's a map, you guys!"

Hunter and Cassy have joined them now, wiping sauce off their faces.

"That star, the memorial, kind of looks like the fancy compass things they put on maps," Cassy observes.

Nodding, Sam's eyes widen. "Maybe it's just

a fancy version of 'X marks the spot,'" she suggests, her voice low. When John and Hunter look at her questioningly, she sighs and then tucks her legs up under her, settling in to tell them the whole story.

Before she's done, John is already on his laptop, running searches. "Her uncle Peter isn't quite the businessman he likes everyone to believe he is," he says after only a few minutes.

"What do you mean?" Sam asks, already chiding herself for not thinking to look into the man further.

"He lost out on a huge investment four years ago, when a business he was CEO of went bankrupt. It was a big scandal that made the papers, but apparently, he still had enough to keep afloat until the whole Eye of Orion Thing."

"What was the name of the business?" Sam asks, suspicious.

"Umm ... all it says is the stock name, Stuart Enterprise. Hang on; let me do another search using that name."

Sam taps at her knee. She knows that name. Where has she heard it before?

"Michael Stuart Enterprise, a horse farm over

in Idaho," John announces. "According to this article, he was indicted on a bunch of racketeering and fraud claims. Although he was never found guilty of anything, it was enough to force him out of business."

"Michael Stuart!" Sam exclaims, finally placing the name. "He was the main ranch hand that took off and abandoned Lisa's aunt."

"What a snake!" Cassy hisses. "And Peter Covington, too. How could Peter do that to his own niece? He had to have lured Michael away by offering him enough money to start his own business."

"That's horrible!" Ally agrees. "But karma got him in the end."

"Maybe," Sam says. "But somehow, Peter Covington still managed to land on his feet. Then, a year later, he sets Lisa up for the heist and collects his millions. Now, when *that* scam is threatened, he comes back to try and make sure it stays covered up."

"I don't get why Lisa doesn't go to the police with all of this," Hunter says, going back for more pizza.

"She's scared," Cassy tells him. "She always

blamed herself for the theft, and now she's convinced that Peter has some way to make the authorities believe she was in on it. I really think she'd rather just forget about it all. While the money would come in handy, it's really painful to accept that her own uncle is doing this to her, not to mention what a scandal like that could do to her reputation as a teacher."

"Except he's made it clear that he doesn't think of himself as her uncle," Sam adds. "Which is another reason she probably hasn't tried to turn him in. She has the Covington name, but legally, she can't prove who she is. The only reason she's even in the house is because of her Aunt Clara. Without those documents, she doesn't really have a legal identity."

"Maybe if we tell her about this new info on Peter, she'll reconsider," Ally says hopefully.

"Maybe," Sam agrees. "It definitely makes him look more suspicious, but what we *really* need to prove it is the Eye of Orion."

"And the documents, so that she can get her inheritance," Cassy states.

"We can't talk to her tonight," Ally points out. "She's at the birthday party at her Aunt's house, remember? She won't be back until late."

Glancing up at the clock, Sam looks back down at the drawing. She and Ally then stare at each other briefly, before breaking out in wide grins.

"Uh-oh," John moans. "I've seen those looks before. Why don't you wait until tomorrow to go treasure hunting, so Hunter and I can go with you?" The two boys have their own birthday party to go to that evening, for one of their mutual friends on the football team.

"It's probably nothing," Sam says, trying to placate the older boy. "I'll bet Jack Covington just tied in the family memorial because it has special meaning, but we have to be sure. It's the only lead we've had so far, and probably our only chance of convincing Lisa of anything. I'd like to explore it before we talk to her tomorrow."

"It's not even five yet," Cassy says, excited. "If we leave now, we should be able to get back before dark, right? How far is it on the trail to the memorial?"

"Less than an hour," Sam says, jumping up. "Sorry guys," she adds, turning to her brother and John. "Have fun at your party!"

Running across the room, Ally stops in front of her parents, explaining that they'd like to go on a quick hike up at the ranch.

"I don't know," Elizabeth replies, hesitating. "I thought those trails were off limits."

"Lisa gave us permission to go on them whenever we want," Ally tells her mom. "Her aunt put those signs out to keep the hunters away."

"Well, as long as you're back before it gets dark," Mr. Parker says, ending the discussion.

Their stomachs protesting at the exercise so soon after eating, the girls pedal their bikes as hard as they can. It starts getting dark around eight, so even if they hurry, it's going to be cutting it close.

They ride in silence for over fifteen minutes, concentrating on reaching their goal as fast as possible. Once there, they drop their bikes at the edge of the driveway in a now familiar routine and gather in an eager huddle near the archway.

"What do you think we're going to find?" Cassy asks, untying her sweatshirt from around her waist and pulling it over her head. The afternoon was warm, but it's already starting to cool off.

"Maybe nothing," Sam answers. "Or maybe everything. Think about it. Jack Covington put a *map* on his daughter's horse, a horse named Orion. The house has been searched several times, without a trace of anything. It would make sense that if Mr. Covington had the ruby, he would keep it somewhere on his property, somewhere safe. But he would also want to make sure that he left a way for his daughter to find it. The memorial, a *family* memorial, would be the perfect place to hide a family heirloom."

"We better hurry," Ally urges, her eyes big as she looks around at the woods and gathering shadows.

What she *doesn't* see are the two men who are standing silently up around the next bend in the driveway, listening to their conversation with great interest.

20

BIRTHRIGHT

The trail is so overgrown that it slows the girls down. Sam leads the way. Although she's wearing jeans and is careful, she still ends up brushing both of her hands against stinging nettles in her attempts to push back the foliage.

The green leafy plant loves the damp climate provided in the Pacific Northwest, especially here, close to the coast. The girls are all too familiar with its bite, and are usually good at avoiding it. Sam waves both of her hands in the air as she walks, and takes deep breaths while her eyes water. She knows the initial pain will fade after a few minutes, but at first, it's always intense.

Ally is impressed at her best friend's toughness. She would likely be hopping around and screaming if it happened to her. She's despised the nettles ever since she was little and was traumatized by them after running into a cluster and falling face-first. It was a nightmare, and even now, she's feeling extremely anxious just knowing that the plant is at her feet.

"It's not that much farther," Sam calls back over her shoulder. "I recognize this big tree up here. Remember, Ally? We used to go inside it and pretend it was our house."

The old cedar tree stands out among its peers; its trunk is massive and twisted. It split at some point, forming two sections that then later bent back and grew together, causing a large alcove. It's inviting to both critters and kids to explore its shadows.

"You're right!" Ally agrees, relieved. It's barely six, but seems much later this deep in the woods.

Less than five minutes later, the narrow trail drops down a steep bank, and then ends at a gigantic rock. Just past the rock is the equivalent of a cliff, looking out to the east. The valley floor spreads out before them, ending as impressive peaks paint a jagged skyline. These are the foothills of the Cascade Mountains.

"What an amazing view!" Cassy admires, leaning against the rock. "I can see why Mr. Covington chose this location for a memorial."

Reading the plaque that's attached to the rock at face level, Cassy crosses her arms. "So it's for his parents. That makes sense. But I don't see any sign of the gem."

Sam steps forward and runs a ringer over the oxidized, brass plate. It's been there for around twenty years. Lisa said she was three when they built the ranch with the inheritance money, and then her grandma died less than two years later. She turns twenty-six tomorrow.

Removing the backpack she brought along, Sam digs around in the pockets. Taking out a small flashlight, she hands that to Ally, who is happy to have it. Opening up the last side pocket, Sam finally smiles with satisfaction. "Here it is!" she shouts, pulling out a Swiss Army Knife.

"Sam, why do you carry around a flashlight

and pocket knife?" Cassy questions, her expression puzzled.

Laughing, Sam flips out the screwdriver attachment, and begins working on the first screw in the plaque. "It's not my school backpack, Cassy. I know better than to take a pocketknife to school! It's my old camping backpack. I keep all my camping gear in it, and I grabbed it to throw my overnight stuff in when Ally invited us to stay the night."

Satisfied with the explanation, Cassy then focuses on what Sam is doing. "Oh!" she exclaims, understanding now. "Good idea, Sam!"

Ally steps in close and turns the flashlight on, making it easier for Sam to see the tiny screws. There are only four of them, and in minutes, the plaque comes away in her hands. Being careful to put the screws in her jeans pocket first so she doesn't lose them, Sam then turns the plaque over. The three girls lean forward, their foreheads touching above it.

"I can't believe it!" Cassy shouts, when she sees the etching on the back.

"What does it say?" Ally demands, unable to read it because the words are upside down from her angle.

"Hold the light higher," Sam directs, tipping the small piece of metal to catch the light.

"The bond of a family is that of love, not blood. Down this trail of life, we end at a place of rest, where a gift is adorned with luck. The same luck that guards our home, and holds our precious daughter close."

After a moment, Cassy breaks the silence. "I don't get it."

Ally turns to Cassy, briefly blinding her with the flashlight before turning it off. "I don't either. I mean, it kind of makes sense, about family and all, but it seems like there's a message there that I don't understand. What gift? What's all the talk about luck?"

Sam's face suddenly brightens, and she pulls the soiled napkin with the doodle from her back pocket. Ally recognizes the look, and her stomach stirs with excitement. Sam is onto something.

Taking the flashlight, Sam turns it back on, shining it on the drawing. Down this trail," she murmurs, tracing the line that continues down from the star that marks the rock they're standing at. "Ends at a place of rest!" she finishes, stretching her arm out to point down the hill. "Where does this trail *start* down there, you guys?"

"The cemetery!" Cassy is the first to reply, making the connection.

"Oh my gosh, I think you're right!" Ally agrees, smiling. "But how does that help us?"

"Come on!" Sam shouts, already running down the hill. "It's less than ten minutes from here."

Ally and Cassy scramble to catch up, trying not to stumble over the exposed roots and branches. Fortunately, it's soon obvious that visitors to the city park, making the plight up to the lookout, still use this bottom portion of the trail. The hike is much easier because of this, and they reach the entrance in just over five minutes.

"The gate is still open!" Sam hollers, not slowing down as she veers from the trail and towards the wide gravel walkway of the cemetery.

Once at the entrance, Sam finally stops, leaning over with her hands on her knees, and breathing heavily. Looking back, she waits for Ally and Cassy, straightening up when they reach her.

"Why are we here?" Cassy asks warily. Although she comes here once a year, she avoids it the rest of the time, and would rather not go in now.

"Do you really think the ruby is going to be *here*?" Ally asks, still catching her breath. "Are the Covingtons buried here?"

"No," Sam answers, already walking again. "I'm pretty sure Lisa mentioned something about a family plot. I don't think they're here."

"Then why are *we* here?" Cassy repeats, following at a distance. When she sees where Sam is headed though, her pace quickens.

When they stop, the three girls are standing in front of the ornate headstone for Cassy's mom. Sam snaps on the flashlight, and directs its beam of light towards the bottom portion of the glittering marble, highlighting the horseshoe.

"Where a *gift* is adorned with luck!" Ally gasps, looking at Sam and then Cassy. "Didn't you say this was donated by someone anonymously?"

Nodding slowly, Cassy just stares. "Why would Jack Covington donate a headstone to *my* mom, and then include it on some weird riddle?"

she asks quietly.

Sam turns the plaque around that she's still carrying and reads it again.

"The bond of a family is that of love, not blood. Down this trail of life, we end at a place of rest, where a gift is adorned with luck. The same luck that guards our home, and holds our precious daughter close."

Gasping, Sam looks up sharply, the flashlight splaying random light across the cemetery. "I know where it's at!" she declares, her eyes blazing bright. "I know where he put The Eye of Orion!"

21

THE WEB WE WEAVE

"Sam, wait!" Ally calls out. Grabbing Cassy's hand, she pulls the other girl along as they race to reach Sam, who is already out of the cemetery. Sam skids to a stop in the gravel, and looks back at them impatiently.

"Shouldn't we, like, search the headstone for another clue or something?" Cassy asks, smiling at an older couple walking by with a bouquet of flowers.

"No," Sam says bluntly, already walking again. "We don't need to." Pulling her cell phone out of her back pocket, she checks the time and then taps briefly at the screen. "Come on!" she urges, putting it away again. "It's going to be dark soon."

"You know something about my mom that you aren't telling me," Cassy says slowly, her eyes narrowed.

Sam turns and makes her way back to Cassy, who is standing with her arms crossed over her chest. Placing a hand on either shoulder, Sam meets her steady gaze. "Cassy, I don't know anything for sure. Yes, I have an idea, but I'd hate to say it and be wrong. Please … can you trust me?"

Cassy stares at Sam, weighing her words. It's been a very long time since Cassy was able to trust anyone, but she knows that Sam would never do anything to hurt her. Nodding slowly, she unfolds her arms and then rocks back off her heels. "We better go!"

The three girls run together in the fading light, going single file back up the pathway to the memorial, and then plunging into the thicker woods. Owls are beginning to call to each other, their voices easily mistaken for other, more mysterious creatures.

Sam concentrates on her breathing, focusing on it and the tempo that their feet make while pounding into the dirt of the forest floor. Taking the lead again, she makes sure to hold her hands up high this time, the redness that's still present a fresh reminder of the danger.

The trek back seems to go faster, and Sam is surprised when they reach the trailhead. Stumbling out onto the blacktop, she almost falls down before staggering to a stop. Ally and then Cassy crash into her back, their legs too tired to respond fast enough to avoid the collision.

Laughing, the three of them catch each other, and then stand huddled, bent over and gasping for air.

Still feeling an urgency that she doesn't quite understand, Sam fumbles with the flashlight, afraid for a moment that the batteries are dead. Hitting the side of it into the palm of her hand, it finally sputters to life. Relieved, she steps back from the other girls and trains it up onto the archway that they're standing under.

Curious as to why Sam is being so cryptic, Ally is about to demand that she explain herself, when she notices *where* Sam is shining the light.

The horseshoe!

"Of course!" Cassy exclaims, all the pieces falling into place for her at the same time. "Jack Covington would have had this made at the same time that he built the ranch. The C in the sign is a horseshoe. The same design as the one on my mom's grave!'

Shaking her head in astonishment, Ally smiles approvingly at Sam and quotes the last sentence of the engraving.

"The same luck that guards our home, and holds our precious daughter close."

Grinning back, Sam lowers the flashlight before turning it off. "We have to see what's inside that horseshoe."

Suddenly, the darkness that's been creeping around them is pushed back by an intense light. Shocked, the girls turn as one towards the head of the driveway, where a car sits with its high beams on. In their excitement, they failed to notice it in the shadows.

"Yes, Sam," Peter Covington's voice booms from the darkness. "I agree. We really *do* need to see what's inside it."

More headlights fall on the scene, but this

time from the other direction. Turning to look for its source, Sam sees a large truck lumbering up the drive, coming from the ranch. It's pulling a horse trailer.

It stops less than ten feet from where they stand. Once dark and silent, the door opens and a large man steps out. It isn't Mr. Hartford, but a middle-aged guy with a broad face and mean eyes.

Fear stirs in Sam's chest, making it hard to breathe. But when the distinct whiny of a horse erupts from the trailer, the fear turns to anger. "That's Orion!" she shouts, looking from the stranger to Peter. "What are you doing with him?"

"That's not your concern," the large man says menacingly, coming around to stand at the front of the truck, mere feet away from Sam.

Sam has her hands in her back pockets, trying to appear relaxed, but her resolve wavers. Ally and Cassy edge in closer, standing behind her. Their increasing fear is palpable.

"Michael's right," Peter agrees, stepping forward so that the girls are now effectively blocked from both directions. "None of this is any of your business. It's a family matter. But … since you've insisted on sticking your head where it doesn't belong, you may as well make yourselves useful. I can't let you run off and go tell stories before securing that ruby, can I?"

Michael! Sam stares back at the man, knowing he must be the former ranch hand who abandoned Lisa to go start a new business with Peter Covington. The same one that went bankrupt because of the shady stuff he was doing. Now, he's trying to steal Orion! Pretending to be scared, she stuffs her hands in her sweatshirt and turns away from Peter, her head down.

Grinning, Peter waves his hands at the girls. "Come on!" he shouts. "Don't let me stop you from your little escapade. Climb up there and get it. Once I have The Eye of Orion, it won't matter *what* my niece says. Because if she tries to expose me, I have some *evidence* that will ensure she goes to jail. Is that what you want?"

Whether it's random, or because the horse hears his name, Orion picks this moment to start kicking at the side of the horse trailer. The racket is startling and Sam, who's already been slowly edging her way towards the woods, takes advantage of it.

Breaking out into a sprint, Sam heads for the back of the trailer. Trying hard to remember the sequence of actions she watched Lisa make earlier in the day, Sam pulls at one lever and then twists another, before lifting up on the rod set into the floor.

Michael reaches her as she grabs for the handle to swing the door open, his large hand clamping down on her arm. Just as he yanks her back and away from the trailer, there's a horrific sound as Orion kicks the door, causing it to swing out and collide with the man's left shoulder.

Grunting in pain, Michael stumbles to the side, stunned. Sam lunges in the other direction, barely escaping the hooves of the panicked horse that leaps from the trailer. Neighing loudly, Orion's eyes roll so that the whites flash in the dark. He then crashes into the woods and out of sight.

Michael recovers quickly, again latching onto Sam's arm before she has a chance to run away. Practically dragging her, he pulls her back around the truck and into the light.

Ally and Cassy stare open-mouthed at Sam, speechless. But Peter Covington appears untroubled.

"Let the horse go," he says almost casually to Michael. "We don't need it anymore."

"You mean you couldn't even figure out that all you needed was a picture of the brand, so you were trying to steal the whole *horse*?" Sam surprises herself with the level of mockery in her voice, but she needs to drag this out for as long as possible, before being forced to climb up to the horseshoe.

Peter growls, taking a slow step towards her. His demeanor changes from almost bored, to dangerous. "You know, I'm getting tired of your snobbish attitude. You're going to do what I tell you, and then you're going to run along and keep your mouth *shut*, unless you want to see your dear teacher in jail. Do … you … understand?"

His face moves closer to Sam's with each word until he's less than a foot away. The steel in his eyes is all too clear. She nods slowly, not daring to say anything in return. Her attempts at diversion are over.

Reaching out, Sam first takes Ally's hand and then Cassy's. They walk together until they're standing at the base of the arch. Turning to face them, Sam sees that they are both near tears. She wants to tell them not to worry, but doesn't dare say anything to set Peter off again.

"Cassy," she says, instead. "I think you're tall enough that I might be able to reach the bottom of the R if I sit on your shoulders."

"Okay," Cassy whispers, and kneels down while Ally helps Sam get on her shoulders. Using the side of the arch to help her stand, Cassy is wobbly at first, but then manages to maneuver under the sign.

It takes some stretching, but Sam finally wraps her fingers around the cold metal. It's made out of handcrafted steel, a thick, high-quality material with solid welds on the edges. Grunting, Sam pulls herself up until she's standing on Cassy's shoulders.

Now she's at eye-level with the large top loop of the R, where it dangles from the crook of the horseshoe, turned slightly to represent the C. Squinting, Sam studies it, trying to find anything that looks out of place. At first, panic starts to claw at her throat. What will Peter do if she's wrong, and the ruby isn't here?

Her eyes stinging with the first hint of defeat, Sam takes a deep breath and wipes at the horseshoe, trying to expose any unusual features.

Wait! This sculpture is an accurate depiction of a horseshoe, including the evenly spaced holes around it. There *is* an odd color to the center hole, at the nape of curve, and when Sam wipes at it more, a faint red color is revealed under the dirt and grime of nearly twenty years accumulation.

The Eye of Orion!

Gasping, Sam nearly falls off of Cassy's shoulders. "I found it!" she shouts, happy at first, but then immediately crestfallen. Time is running out. She *can't* let them leave with it!

Looking more closely at the ruby, Sam determines that the horseshoe is hollow, and the jewel is set inside of it, with it showing through the hole on the opposite side. There has to be a way to open it. Stretching as far as she can, Sam runs her hand along the welded seam and then switches to the other side, stopping when she finds a clasp, discreetly set in the crook of the horseshoe.

Holding her breath, Sam presses the release and pushes up gently on the top until it lifts. It creaks in protest, but opens about four inches before being stopped by the top loop of the R. But it's enough. Reaching inside, Sam places her hand over the palm-sized ruby and after fiddling with it briefly, twists it off its base.

"Hurry, Sam!" Cassy groans. "I can't hold you much longer."

Doing her best to not give away her success, Sam switches the large jewel to her left hand to free her right and then focuses on what she suspects to be a more important find. A small metal box, about two by four inches, is nestled in the rest of the space. Gripping it, she lifts it out and holds it close to her chest.

"Here it is!" Sticking her left hand out so that the headlights catch the color of the jewel, Sam waves it around dramatically, while discreetly sliding the box down into the large front pocket of her sweatshirt, where her phone also rests.

The distraction works, but almost too well. Cassy looks up, and then staggers back, squealing as she loses her balance. Ally lunges forward, catching Sam and softening the blow as they both hit the ground.

Ignoring the possible injuries, Peter reaches out and yanks the Eye of Orion from Sam's hand. "Finally!" he yells, looking almost maniacal in the yellow cast of the light. "We have it, Michael! Now no one can ever prove that the other was a fraud, and I know plenty of buyers willing to make this one disappear."

Slowly getting to her feet, Sam then helps Ally up, who appears unhurt. They join Cassy, and then try to creep towards the trail.

"What do we do with them?" Michael barks, ignoring the older man's rambling words, and pointing at the cowering girls. "We really aren't going to let them go, are we?"

Cringing at the terrifying meaning behind his words, Sam begins to feel desperate. What has she gotten her friends into?

"What we're going to do is…"

Peter's words are cut off by a crashing from the woods. They all turn towards the dark trail as Orion plunges out onto the road and heads directly for Peter!

Peter throws his hands up to protect himself

as the huge Arabian horse collides with him. Orion barely slows before continuing forward, as Peter is launched through the air, the Eye of Orion spiraling in an arc in the opposite direction.

Everyone else is frozen in shock, but Sam is spurred into motion before the collision is even over. Her eyes riveted on the jewel, she leaps forward and catches it just before it hits the ground!

"Go!" Sam shouts to Ally and Cassy, after rolling to a crouching position. "Run!"

The two other girls head for the trail behind them, but Sam is cut off by Michael, who steps in her way. Stretching a hand out towards her, he tilts his head and then makes a 'come here' motion.

Sam looks at her fleeing friends, down at the moaning form of Peter Covington, and then back at the menacing man before her, trying to decide what to do next. But before she can make a decision, the space around them is suddenly filled with the flashing of red and blue lights!

22

A FAMILY DEFINED

"I still don't understand how you did it," Ally whispers sleepily to Sam. The girls are sitting together on the same sofa they shared the week before, in the den of Covington Ranch.

"Well, like I told you, I texted my mom before we left the cemetery and told her we were going to be at the ranch," Sam replies, tapping her foot impatiently. They've been waiting there for over an hour now, while the police finish speaking with all of their parents and Lisa.

"When Peter Covington first showed up, I snuck my phone into my sweatshirt. When I turned my back on him, I was able to look at the screen briefly, but the text was short and garbled. I'm glad my mom was able to figure out that we needed the police."

"It did the trick," Cassy observes. She's standing at the window, staring out at the strobing lights. She wonders, briefly, why they haven't turned them off. The two men were carted away a while ago.

"Well, I'm learning," Sam laughs. "There's a reason why our parents want to always know where we are!"

"*Especially* with you!" Ally pokes good-naturedly.

"I'm sure the department will do a three day investigative hold," a loud voice announces, breaking into their conversation. It belongs to the sheriff, a tall, robust, middle-aged man. He enters the room with a group of avid listeners behind him.

"After that, it will be up to the judge to determine which charges to bring against them." Turning so that he can address their parents and Lisa, who followed him in, he spreads his hands wide. "The whole family ruby thing is likely an issue that the original insurance company will pursue. We're going to be looking at robbery, since they used force to try to steal the horse. Michael Stuart will also be cited for resisting arrest, plus assault for grabbing Sam. Both men will be charged for holding the girls against their will." The sheriff looks down at the girls when he says this.

"You're lucky, Sam, that no one was seriously hurt tonight," the sheriff says. When Sam opens her mouth to protest, he adds quickly, "I know, you weren't doing anything wrong. Just do me a favor. Next time, when you think you know the whereabouts of a multi-million dollar item that questionable men are also hunting for, tell your parents instead of trying to get it yourself. Okay?"

Blushing now, Sam can't think of anything to say to counter his logic. Instead, she simply nods.

"Alright, I think this belongs to you," the officer continues. Stepping next to Lisa, he pulls the Eye of Orion from his front breast pocket and hands it to her. "I would suggest contacting the insurance company first thing Monday morning." Tipping his hand to the side of his forehead in a salute, he makes his exit.

Lisa is speechless as she holds the large, star cut ruby. Although it's covered in a layer of dirt, it's still luminescent.

Kathy Wolf sits down next to Sam, her freckles standing out against her pale skin. Putting an arm around her daughter, she gives her a squeeze. "You sure you're okay?" she asks, studying Sam's face.

"Yeah, Mom. I'm sorry for scaring you like this. Where are the twins?"

"Across the street at Mrs. Kirkpatrick's. She was happy to take care of them for me."

Sam watches as Lisa turns the gem over in her hands several times, and then notices that Cassy is still standing in front of the big picture window. Her back is to them, almost as if she's reluctant to turn around.

"Did you bring it?" Sam asks her mom, her voice low.

Kathy nods, and lifts her canvas shoulder bag onto her lap. Reaching in, she withdraws Cassy's small shoebox. It was one of the few items from her home that she brought to Sam's. "Are you sure about this?" Kathy cautions.

Sam gave her mom a quick summary of

events earlier, when she first called her after the police arrived. While Kathy knows there may be something important in the box, she doesn't know what it is.

Brandon and Elizabeth Parker look tired, and motion for Ally to come with them, but before Ally can respond, there's a fresh commotion from the foyer, and Lisa's Aunt Clara makes a grand entrance.

"Lisa!" she exclaims, running up to her niece. "I *told* the sheriff that man was a scoundrel! Maybe now he'll believe me. What in the world happened?"

"He figured out that Orion was a key to where the ruby was," Lisa says, directing Clara to one of the high-backed chairs. "So he and Michael came up here and stole him while I was away!"

"But Sam was way ahead of him," Ally says proudly. She sneaks a sideways glance at her parents, and is relieved to see that they've found chairs to sit in, apparently deciding to stay a while longer.

Clara listens intently as Lisa retells the whole story. Sam steps forward to give her the plaque at one point, and then Lisa reveals the Eye of Orion, nestled in her palm.

"So it was here all along," Clara breathes, her eyes transfixed by the gem. "But, Sam," she questions, directing her attention to the young girl with some effort. "I don't understand the connection between Cassy's mother's headstone and the ranch. How in the world could you have figured that out?"

Cassy finally turns from the window, and the mixture of confusion and hope on her face is too much for Sam. Whether she's right or wrong, she *has* to tell Lisa what she suspects, and let her determine if it's true.

"There were all sorts of clues," Sam admits, stuffing her hands in her sweatshirt pocket. "I didn't realize it until tonight in the cemetery. But," she says hastily, approaching Lisa, "Before we talk about that, I think it's important for you to see this." Pulling out the small tin box, Sam hands it to Lisa. "This was also in the horseshoe, but I hid it while everyone was distracted by the ruby because …" Pausing, Sam runs her hands through her hair, anxious to see its contents. "I think what's inside is more valuable to you than

The Eye of Orion."

Her eyes wide, Lisa's face brightens as comprehension forces a huge smile. She eagerly snaps open the old box, and withdraws several sheets of folded paper. Everyone leans forward, watching intensely as Lisa carefully unfolds the brittle documents.

"Is it?" Clara is the first to ask, her voice thick. "Have we finally found the adoption papers?"

Nodding, her eyes welling with tears, Lisa quickly scans the top sheet and then the second. "They're from an attorney's office in a town a couple hundred miles from here," she explains. "It's mostly legal jargon, but it outlines the agreement and terms of the adoption. The last paper here is a copy of what must be my birth certificate. It simply lists 'baby girl', for a name, but the birthday is the same as mine. Tomorrow!"

Sam's head snaps up at this, and a shiver of anticipation races along her spine. Going back to her mom, she picks up the shoebox. When Cassy sees it, her eyes get big, and she tilts her head questioningly at Sam.

"Are you going to tell me now?" she asks, her voice hoarse and demanding.

Lisa tears herself away from the adoption papers at the sound of Cassy's tormented plea. When she sees what Sam is holding, she looks back and forth between the two girls. "What's going on?" she asks Sam, confused.

"Cassy," Sam says, ignoring Lisa for the moment, "You told me that your mom dropped out of school and moved away when she was sixteen. Did your grandma ever tell you why?" When Cassy shakes her head no, Sam opens the box. "You also said that she eventually made it into college and was married right after she graduated, but then died a short time later at the age of thirty, less than a year after you were born."

Ally is listening to Sam in rapt anticipation. If Sam is suggesting what Ally thinks, this is bigger than any mystery they've ever solved ... and much more important.

Gently, Sam moves things around in the shoebox, and then pulls out the old papers she'd briefly looked at the other night while in Cassy's room. "You've thought all this time that this birth certificate is your mom's, because it has her name on it. But I don't think it is." Offering the paper to Lisa, Sam holds her breath until the older woman takes it. "It *does* have her name on it, but the date is wrong. That's been bugging me, and I think that now I know why."

Lisa is silent while studying the certificate, but her face changes from curious to amazement, and then shock, as she looks back and forth between it and the one from the tin box. "These are the same!" she chokes out, after forcing the words around a very large lump in her throat. "I believe that Cassy's is the original, and this one," she says incredulously, waving the other paper, "Is a copy of it."

"But how can that be?" Clara demands, staring at Cassy. The young girl appears frozen, her face pale.

"The only other signature on the adoption paper besides my parents," Lisa interrupts, looking again at the paperwork, "Is someone named, Anita Sue Tipton."

A sharp intake of breath causes everyone to look at Cassy. Tears are already spilling down her cheeks. "That's Grams," she whispers, wrapping her arms around herself as if cold.

"If Cassy's mom were a minor, then Grams would have likely signed the paperwork as her legal guardian," Kathy offers as an explanation.

Sam gasps as the reality sinks in. This *has* to mean that Cassy's mom had another child, back when she was only sixteen. She gave her up for adoption, which was discreetly arranged between Grams and the Covingtons. Lisa was Cassy's half-sister!

"That's why Grams moved us back here," Cassy says aloud to herself. "And why she was so obsessed with the Covingtons. She knew all along!" With that declaration, her voice gains strength, and Cassy looks up at Lisa, a kind teacher she met just a few weeks ago and has grown to admire. A woman who now meant so much more.

"Thanks to Sam, I have what I need to unlock my inheritance and restore the ranch," Lisa announces loudly to everyone in the room. But in a surprise gesture, the new heiress turns and tosses the long sought after documents carelessly aside. Shaking her head, she walks up to Cassy and takes her hands in her own.

"But those papers mean nothing in comparison to what else we've discovered," Lisa states. "My dad was right. The bond of a family *is* love, and I believe he meant for us to find each other, Cassy. You're my sister, and neither one of us will ever be alone again."

Cassy finally allows herself to believe what's happening, and walks into the open embrace that Lisa offers. The two sisters hug each other, holding on tightly to the family they've both dreamt of for so many years.

Ally steps up happily to Sam's side, wrapping an arm around her shoulders. The two friends look at each other, both at a loss for words. They've been through some exciting escapades together, but this one is different.

Sam is relieved to have solved the mystery of the ranch, and located the Eye of Orion, but the *real* treasures are the sisters that have been reunited!

THE END

Thank you for reading, *The Heiress of Covington Ranch!* I hope that you enjoyed it, and will take the time to write a simple review on Amazon!

http://www.amazon.com/dp/B011H7SG0K

Want to be notified when Tara releases a new novel? Sign up now for her newsletter! eepurl.com/bzdHA5

Be sure to look for Sam and Ally in other exciting adventures in *The Samantha Wolf Mysteries!*

ABOUT THE AUTHOR

Author Tara Ellis lives in a small town in beautiful Washington State in the Pacific Northwest. She enjoys the quiet lifestyle with her two teenage kids, and several dogs. Having been a firefighter/EMT and working in the medical field for many years, she now teaches CPR and concentrates on family, photography and writing young adult novels.

Made in the USA
Monee, IL
18 October 2020